A Day at the O

A Day at the Office

Robert Alan Jamieson

Polygon
EDINBURGH

© Robert Alan Jamieson 1991

First published by Polygon
22 George Square
Edinburgh

Set in Linotron Sabon
by Koinonia, Bury
Printed and bound by
Redwood Press, Melksham, Wiltshire

British Library Cataloguing in Publication Data

Jamieson, Robert Alan
A day at the office
I. Title
823'.914[F]

ISBN 0 7486 6099 2

The publisher acknowledges subsidy from the Scottish Arts Council towards the publication of this volume.

The reality of this work is a product of the imagination.

* * *

Without art, the crudeness of reality would be unbearable.

George Bernard Shaw

These are times when what is to be said looks out of the past at you — looks out like someone at a window and you in the street as you walk along. Past hours, past acts take on an uncanny isolation; between them and you who look back on them now there is no continuity.

opening of *Young Adam* by Alexander Trocchi

Imagine there's no heaven

John Lennon

Page one: Zero (the fool)

This book is a day and a night in the life of a Scottish city, seen through the imaging eye of a dreaming worker, who conjures to life the novel's three motor characters - Ray, age nineteen; Helen, twenty-four, and Douglas, twenty-nine. Their connection is brief, yet inevitable in the fact that they are all parts of the single psyche, that of the dreamer/conjuror. The conjuror or magician, le bateleur, *is the first enigma in the sequence of symbols known as the major arcana of the Tarot. It is the magician who produces these images of the subconscious, his alter egos. Each of these characters have separate readings. Ray's seven cards are* la papesse, les amoureux, l'hermite, la force, temperance, l'etoile, *and* jugement. *Helen's seven cards are* l'empereur, le chariot, la roue de fortune, la mort, le diable, la lune, le monde. *Douglas has* l'empresse, le pape, le just, le pendu, le maison dieu, le sol, *and* le monde. *Together they add up to a system for an understanding of the psychic journey, as symbolised by the Tarot, specific to a fixed locality in timespace.*

The worker is the magician. History is their invention, their realisation of the city they live in. The interior monologue of the narrator/dreamer fuses with the mind of the others engaged in the same dreaming. Together they invent society. And it is here, at the point of conjunction between the parallel worlds of reality and imagination, that the curiously crucial hinge between fiction and experience operates. This interface is central to our intelligence, and the sense we make of our lives, as crucially placed in our thought as zero, which hinges the sense of plus and minus numbers, of absence and presence.

In fiction, the art of dreaming/imagining as narrative reaches its highest point. Imagined worlds are created with their own dynamics, to exemplify or portray ideas about the realised world of experience.

The essential function of imagination in all areas of human existence, the ways in which the power and status of the dreaming art emerge in human society, are evidenced everywhere. In the extreme case, the aboriginal culture of Australia holds that the dream contains reality and there is no need to make things other, for they are eternally perfect anyway. In Indian philosophy, the material is merely an illusion, while true reality has no material form. Therefore material hardship is not a problem to be solved but a test to be endured.

Now, in consumerist society, wish-fulfilling fantasies are manufactured to stimulate and amuse us in our dull moments, to keep us awake to the fullest potentials of the imaginative craft, while simultaneously subduing a rebellion of the heart away from capitalist concerns: the materialist attempt to convince that dreams too are at a price.

The artless reality of late 20th century life can be so tedious that it sends us spinning to invention of other worlds. The day at the office or the factory has become such a deadening intellectual experience for the millions who endure the role of underling, that they are prepared to subsidise those among us who are paid to dream in lieu of others.

So art enters the factory and the office, to reinterpret old stories into new guises, to retell the myths of the great tribe of sapiens sapiens, *to chart its manifold evolution from out of our pasts, into this arid future. The search for a new significance for the work and a new way of presenting it goes on, not merely a further ornamentation upon a fixed and immutable mythology, but a reshaping of the myth itself, a fundamental shaking of the life tree. Is it possible? Dont doubt it: it is necessary ...*

0430
this is the dream I'm having
the moonwise children
go under
the bridge
to the other side

this is the dream
it's perfectly lucid
almost superreal
when you get inside

it's in three colours
youll tell them apart
with ease
though they shade
into oneanother
become mixed
become me
though they go about the city
crossing streets
in cars
they are conjured
out of shadows
by the sleeping motion
of the dreamer me

It
begins with a funeral
with death
with the end of MINE YOURS
HERS HIS ITS
THEIRS
names replace the metaphors
though the metaphors really
matter

                    Instead of matter
                 there is this web of language
                     that enfolds us
                           and
                 we have forgotten how to look
                 at things without naming them
                   the hardest things to deal
                  with are these spaces between
                         the words

                      Yetwereallydoneedthem

                         and names

                   for conventions and people
                  make more conventional people
                            i
                          oh i
                            I
                          i ray
                          -Ray-
roll the dice
                 if the dream is to be dreamt at all really
                         let's get lost
                          you and I
                       get to know me
                            merge
                            be me
                        emerging as
                          'Helen'
take a card any card
                       the dreaming incants
                            names
                           creates
                             ME
                            Born
                         «Douglas»
say the magic works
                    badabra   abraca
                           speak

A Day at the Office

the brother of the other. I cry a lot. The world is white and reaching out for that hand. And this is how it will always feel now, now that Hugh is dead. Little red corduroy trousers, bib and brace, both of them, Hugh bigger always stronger, submit. SUBMIT or I'll break your podgy little fingers. This was the first Hugh. Then it was here have a smoke. It's ok, man. What are you, a kid still. The world's outhere and it's happening now, boy. Hee hee.

The dead can still laugh. Through you, wee impulses. Talking too. If I were still alive. Their father's funeral. Black day. Crows and ravens. Without the benefit of last minute absolution. A happydrunk. A happy deaddrunk. Dead.

Hugh. That bike he had, the one I couldnt ride. Remember the chain came off that time and he blamed me. But it was an accident, I didnt do it. He gave me a chinese burn. Swine.

Is that singular or plural? Like you maybe. Never sure.

Here it comes now. The earth. Thank goodness I dont have to lift that box again. Get ready drop the cord into the hole. Christ this is really it. Religious swears. Worst kind. The shovel. What's she doing? Crying? Roy Orbison. It's over.

IT'S OVER

1965, I was seven – or was it eight? Funny, forgetting like that. But the song stays there, really clear Top of the Pops, just before Laramie. Cowboys, up at the ganghut, the tree. Bikes lying on their sides among the autumn leaves. Piaf..... sad lives. But never flat lives. Eruptions.

Comes of living near ley lines perhaps. Ask Stuart. Wonder why he didnt come? Was it her? The bereaved mother. Maybe. Do I hate her? Could any son? Maybe. Kill them sometimes, if they're overly maternal.

Minister looked at me oddly earlier. Probably only the transmission of some divine compassion in my difficult time.

The clichéd words – dust ashes? Surely something more elemental than that. At least the spirit should: ascend of course. Transcend maybe.

Zen. I'll read Zen. Suzuki. Motorbikes. Buy a motor bike and drive to Spain have an adventure write a travelogue like Stevenson. But locations need to be exotic. Spain's too ordinary. In fact everywhere is now. People should just stay at

home and explore their inner space. Know how it is?
  Zen and the art of motorcycle maintenance. Now I see it. Suzuki. That's the connection, damn to have missed that for all these years. Suzuki satori. The otherness of rapid travelling. Leaving your magnetism in a swirl. Damn. I'll write that down. Have I got paper pen. Cant do it now though, maybe discreetly as we go back towards the cars. I'm with mother. In the back seat with mother. The black seat. Black sheep. Baa baa. Bye bye Hugh, you fucking swine. I loved you.
  That last time. Croaking, old, bitter against everyone. Only thirty-eight. Money. Waiting on the inheritance. But wise in a way. Surviving as long as he did. The last Hugh. Adds up to a life, mother

names

incants She

Helenme

Step back. Dont give so much away. He's asking more from you than he has a right to, Helen me. Yes, I know that I know that's true, I know he's taking from me more than he's prepared to give me in return. But cant just leave him can I

can I? I mean
we're married

I've been with him years. We've sort of grown up together, blended, mixed one into the other. It wouldn't be right.
  Talking to yourself. Healthy, not a sign of madness at all. It's incantation, casting spells. Stroke your cat today.

spell

incants

I will know the right decision when the time comes to make it.

I am not firm in resolution
but will sing in the wind
an Aeolian harp

was that what they called it? Why cant I remember these things. Improve your memory. Concentrate on street maps and bus routes. Get out and about. Find a job. Earn money. Get the paper later. Get it now.
  That's it. There would be nothing Colin could do about it. Not if I had my own money. Then I could just move out and

find a place to live in my own. In the city. I want to be involved in things for a while. I've been out here on the margins for far too long.

I dont want to blame maw. It's not her fault. She was a prisoner of the cultural traditions, she just passed it on blindly to me. But you'd think she would have tried to stop me. Making a mess of things. Stuart.

I'll go and see Stuart. He'll know somebody. Just a room out of here till I get sorted out.

Put a tape on. Music. Calm down. Dont let on. I cant let him see or he'll try and stop me. He'll talk me out of it, with that stupid little boy bit. I need you. Mummy. I dont want to mummy him I want my own life. My own kids. Not with him.

Not that I dont care for him. I must do to have lasted this long. Or is it habit?
          monks hood habits
      spooky like big woolly pricks
        when the hood is up
Wheugh, horrible even to think of it, symbols of masculinity. Thing is they dont see. Men are simple. Too busy looking in the mirror. Or the polished wong of the car. Did I say wong? Thinking about cooking. Wok. Chinese. Take away, I'll phone get them to bring it. Free delivery from the Yangtse River. Think of it all that distance. Lucky they dont have to go home at night
        habit
That's the way they think about them round here. Bigots. Catch myself at it sometimes. In the atmosphere, differences. Men women, black white. Why does it have to be that way round.

Right. Switch off. I'd miss this carpet I suppose. Remember going to choose it. What a laugh that was. And then his brother-in-law spilling the red wine at the housewarming. Had to move the couch. Still over it. Wonder if I should bother getting it cleaned properly. I mean you see these things advertised but do they work? Worth more if I could get the stain out. That's something. That's the door.

God that hoover rings in your head. COMING

conjures
bears
names∆∆∆∆∆incants
the even three: gemini
sun ray tips. sun ray tips. sunray tips. tea for yer maw tea for yer maw sunray tips tea for yer maw. Ha ha. Skipping ropes used to whirr here then. Girls bare legs only little but sometimes their knickers.

Ray Ray. Come on son. Control it. Cool out lad. Marie Wee Marie. She married that optician she worked for, moved out. Pretty girl, clever too though not intelligent. Ignorant maybe just. That was the thing round here, people didnt have the same chance. You had to leave your world behind to become a scholar
foreign language english
Language of domination
Fuck them
write up in red spray
metallic
decorate with gold
edding 75 if enough time
English language of domination. LANGUAGE OF DOMINATION. But who'd get the point? Better with FUCK THE ENGLISH BASTARDS. Get the footsoldiers on the march.

Christ this PARKS FULL OF FUCKING DOGSHIT. Bastard. Right up the side. Need to find a docken or something. Jeesus would you believe. Dogs ought to be fucking shot anyway, strays half of them. Like the old man told me about the dog packs in Piraeus. Fancy that this summer.

Greece.

Work my way. Grape picking. Beer festivals. Save some callydosh. Lie on the beach for while. Still gotta get the fare together though. Could be a problem. Take a giro an go? Could be better have some capital.

Nick something maybe, sell it? Need to be big though. Video or something. Fuckin dogshit.

Hope this guy's in. Hate to go home without a blow. Can always try Jan.
Jan Gunn,
the shipwrecked soul
Gimme cheese

A Day at the Office

She's a bit mousey too. But sharp teeth, give you a nasty bite. Where did that thing go she gave me, that wee soapstone seal. Must have lost it outside. Or down the couch.
    Footbol the night. Live. Watch it wi the ole guy or go out. Go to a pub where I can watch it. Big screen.
    49.
There's that woman from the Post Office. Part timer. Got held up and threw a complete wobbler, looks fuckin awful. Only aboot forty, knackered on downers. It's this place. Well no me, no get me, me out. Wonder if they smell the dogshit

                  fifty
                  pleas
          take me outa here
             mr busdriver
         mr greyhound man
       you otta know by now
           Imatravellinon
                  man

Bus deck top.
Fag.

        this is the dream
     and the magic it works
   is the logos that act and word
            marry
     turn out your pockets
  and trust to the stone in your
           mouth

0800
ALARM CALL
this is what i do
i dream of bees inside the lion
the syrup tin of samson
the riddle me ree
good morning good morning
this is your early morning
is the answer a joke?
this line the punch?
are you awake yet?
it delivers respectful poison
submits its quiet venom
WORK'S EASY RIGOURS ARE YOUR
LAST SWEET DREAM
though other music plays at
night's death flame
I wont call again
THIS IS YOUR EARLY MORNING
i wake up late
the sleep the answer
the joke on it
pull clothes and self together
stuff morsel into mouth
wash skin awake
outdoor
huh-huh-puff the cold air
bus
stops
change
upstair
my clinging porridged face
clinched grey
the first principle

A Day at the Office

0846
roundabout
the junctions blocked
cars tail back to sleeper towns
my bus top chariot halts
look down from high
ON BOSS CAR
reversing roles
he overseen thus by me
in his shiny Company Vehicle
queuing also for admittance
to the centre
WE IGNORE
each other's compromising stare

0900
passing through the door
summoning the lift
the minute hand to
has the second circled
when will it tock
THE CELEBRATORY INDULGENCE OF
EMOTION
ACCOMPANYING RITUAL ACTION
IN THE UNCOLLECTED MIND
IS THE BASIC BUILDING UNIT
IN THE PROCESS OF SOCIAL
RENEWAL
caught in the merry dance
of being
this same place same time
tomorrow
clockprint **0901**
the black inkmarks read late
A SECOND CHANCE IS NOT AN
OPTION
even if i think i'm due one
THE PUNCHED CARD SHOWS THE
MOMENTS GONE

> we shouldnt have to do this
> repeat repeat repeat
> AFTER ME
> AFTER ME
> we should be free to wander
> free to dream
> like
> ray i Ray

walking across the city, cutting through the lines of traffic, hurrying past shoppers and strollers he hurries towards the park, the rhythm of his footsteps punctuating the music in his mind.

> beatniks
> beat it
> consuming passions
> buy it

A half mile away, across the flat plain, the tenements of Tollcross and the spire of some kirk make a ridge of stone against the sky. He walks along the cycle path under the trees till he comes to the corporation tennis courts. There's nobody about, so he crouches down where the hedges make a corner and takes his tartan dufflebag from his shoulder. He has enough left for a single skinner. The wind makes the rolling tricky but he is expert enough at it to make the spliff without losing anything. It is a ritual, performed in solemn anticipation of the high

> a high like the first, the best

A regular habit, though dealers came and went as folk lost their nerve or were bust. He couldnt imagine living without it. If a drought materialised, as sometimes happened, he was so caught up in the search for it around the city that he didn't stop to think how it felt

> i
> keeps moving
> walking
> on the bus
> in a taxi
> towards the deal
> to the address
> where a bit might be got

to the time when the deal was done and he was on his own, to weigh and sample at his leisure. He smokes the j quickly. The breeze accelerates the burning and he sucks at the cardboard

A Day at the Office

tip eagerly, not wanting to miss a toke. Soon he is pinching the thing between finger and thumb, extracting the ultimate hit. Sad time. Then he gets up from his hideaway and starts out across the cropped grass towards Tollcross. He cant make out the hands on the clocktower
> but it's near enough twenty to
> the signing time

The signing is a ritual too. He doesnt want a real job, just wee things on the side now and then cash in hand, no commitment to anything or a role to play in society. Sometimes
> i catches myself thinking i might be yellow
> not to give it a go

but it was more fun just looking, and he could have talked himself into a job if he wanted to. It isnt that he is shy or afraid of work, it's that kind of limit it would set on his time, the demands that the sense of having to do or be put on him. Now he is free to move about, seeing who he wants to, going where he wants to. That was worth a lot more
> more than a dudwage
> or a daft
> career
> at nineteen
> on the brink is near enough
> you can see all you need to from there
> i got plenty of time

The queue in the dole is short and he pulls the crumpled card from his hip pocket and hands it to the girl behind the counter. She flicks through the box and finds his form and he writes *Ray Craig* on the dotted line with a flourish. Some days it's great. You are in and out like that, before the doom of the place gets a hold of you. Others, well you just got stuck at every set of lights
> hold it
> it's in your hand
> your hand alone the pen that
> writes your name

Ray had some dealing to do. He had enough to buy a teenth but that would leave him broke, so he was planning out a way of getting a smoke and holding onto the cash. He was going up to see Jan. She was a fair bit older than him, but he
> knows her from Craigs
> she is a wise one
> always good to me

checkwatch **0945**
the firstmost yawn dictates
the domino tumble
we tap and push these buttons
SCRIBBLE DOWN IN CARELESS
SCRIPT OF SPIDERS
an eyepiece on the yawning city
these figures of the average
FORM WEBS OF PULSED STATISTICS
netting over every target block
small quantities of lightning
pass through our fingertips
each time we press these keys
this may be the source
of the disorientation in
society:
our bodies are largely water
water and electrics do not mix
YOUR EMPTY HEADS PRODUCE A
DULLING ECHO
SIMPLE abcs OF TIME
SHOULD BE DISTRIBUTED AMONG YOU
to charge our instinct
we should sleep
while the moon
is waxing strong
to charge our instinct
with the electric off
at the main
oh i Ray in stinked
tell me where you go
there's no stair lighting in the close and when the heavy split wood door shuts behind him, Ray's in near darkness
like i wus set down on the other side of the planet
where it was black
night. He groped his way up the winding steps towards a beam of day hard pressed to filter through a filthy skylight. After a second turn of steps, he stood in relative sunshine in front of a door which had upon it pinned a list of names with *Mail for:*

A Day at the Office

at its head. He chapped the door three times, then leant forward to try to see in through the peep-hole fish eye.
The hall seemed to spiral
away to a distance
of a mile
or so
He heard Joe's voice mutter something, then an eye looked out and the chains were unfastened. The door opened. Joe grunted a greeting and turned to call 'It's Ray' down the hallway. Then he shuffled socked feet after his words. The tv was rattling out some high drama
hey you I wanna punch/kiss you
–How's it goin? Ray asked loudly.
–OK
–Anything come for me?
–Naw. No cheque yet if it's that you're lookin for.
  They went into the tv room and Joe sat down on a couch in front of the set. The exhausted springs lapsed with a creak. Jan was sitting on a companion armchair with her feet up on the coffee table, and she pulled a grin and rubbed her fingers through her hair.
–Hiya Ray. How're things?
Ray shrugged – Survivin. Good this?
  She didnt answer. He sat down on a straight backed chair at an angle to the screen so that he caught only two dimensions of the illusion. Jan lit a cigarette, took first a draw and then a sip from a pink flamingo patterned mug at her elbow on an upturned wooden box that doubled as a table
flamingos
dying
poisoned world
uncentred
  After a few seconds she said –Aye, no bad. Seen it afore though. Kirk Douglas is this newspaper reporter who gets this scoop. Some old bloke's stuck down a mine shaft out in the desert. Joe's seen it too but he's forgotten.
–No I've no, Joe muttered.
–Aye you have. I watched it wi you. No mind?
–I've no seen it. Musta been somebody else.
Jan pressed her point. –I watched it wi you.
–I've no fuckin seen it, right? He gave her a dirty look and

she made a face at him, then laughed. He made a big show of ignoring her. She looked at Ray and pointed at Joe.

–He's got a mind like a sieve. Dope stupid, ken what I mean?

Ray crossed his legs and tried to lean back on the chair but it squeaked out a warning.

Joe, who had been sitting beside her on the settee with his legs outstretched toasting sweaty socks on a two bar electric fireglow, glanced away from the telly towards him.

–Watch that chair, man. It's no too safe.

So Ray sat upright again. He waited for a lull in the action on the telly. Kirk Douglas was in the mineshaft
>   eyesablaze with nordic fury,
>   selling the culture down the swannee
>   selling bringing me to buying

–You got anything just now?

Jan didnt answer, she was totally into Kirk's eyes, but Joe took out a small plastic bag from down the side of the couch and tossed it over to him.

–Bit o bush, he said without looking away from the screen

–It's no bad. Ray opened the bag that had once held fifty ps for the meter. He sniffed at the grass inside.

–OK to roll one?

Jan nodded, –Sure.

He began the ritual, using his own papers and tobacco.
>   lick it and stick it
>   different folk in different ways
>   like the Dooman says

When it was complete, he handed the bag back and lit the j. The first taste sent a wave of pleasure through his body.

–Nice, he murmured, then took another draw, then another, till his lungs couldnt hold any more. He passed the spliff to Jan, held the smoke inside as long as he could, then exhaled slowly.

–How much of it you got?

She wagged her head from side to side as she smoked. –Could let you have an eighth.

–How much?

–Call it fifteen?
>   hold what dosh youve got ray
>   grass is ok
>   but

A Day at the Office

you can sell a half of this
and get
a bit of black
a teenth
there's guys to try later

    Ray agreed, –ok till the rent cheque comes? Should be any day.
    She passed the j onto Joe.
    –Aye, ok, Ray.
    Then she got up and left the room. Ray looked at Joe.
    –Load a shite this really.
    –Yeah?
He stretched out his arms above his head making a v shape with his short cut bristle head at its crux. He looked bored

bulldog
sleeping
but always ready to bite

but he was totally engrossed in the film, really. Jan came back carrying another bag like her own. Opening the door, emerging from the dark of a poor winter's light, she was

Cleopatra
clever cattish
highpriestess of her home

a shadow in the shadows. Ray took the bag. They sat silently watching the film and smoking

i've seen this too
this is a classic

    Ray realised, but he didnt say so. The dramatic climax was reached without words from the watchers. When it finished, while the credits were still on the screen, Joe switched channels to a panel game. Celebrity contestants had to guess the identity of mystery celebrity guests. The show was hosted by a comedian, one that Ray recognised as the one that had had the hit record with that kids' song in the seventies.
    –Christ what's his name.
    Joe said –He's a twat whatever his name is, isnt he?
    He laughed, whinnying

good draw this
drawhorse

Pulling at the collar of his shirt, standing up to pass the j, Ray swayed backwards and nearly fell onto the couch on top of Jan. She looked up and laughed.

—Watch yoursel, you.
   Joe said nothing. Didnt take his eyes off the television. Ray sat down again. Ray was getting off on the moment.
   —Gonnæ put this off and put some music on, Jan?
   Joe spoke slowly —I'm watchin this, you.
He seemed to like watching twats on television. He liked watching television
>television head
>dead head
>nip the buds now

Jan sat up —Hey you, it's my telly and I'll put it off if I wantæ, right?
   —Thought I had some rights around here, bein a paying tenant.
   —Social pays your rent, chum.
   —Dinnæ push me. I've just about had it wi you.

>conducted in whispers
>Joes sideswipe glances
>tearing chunks out her
>Jan cool
>ladyathome
>grinningsoul
>while the lad's insane
>in love is to be just that
>in a state of sane
>it's the rest of time we're barmy armies
>oh i
>i ray
>could stay
>with you two
>too

   —Why dont you eh?   —Whit?
   —You know   —Whit?
   —Go?
All this is underlined with looks, these fierce whispers, as Jan and Joe are still pretending not to be as angry as they obviously are for Ray's benefit

>whispers say
>he hits her
>yeah?

   Joe got up all of a sudden, springing to his feet like he'd been jabbed by a hairpin through the flattened springs of the old settee. He stomped over to the door, and went out scowling back as the door swung shut behind him.

Ray looked at Jan. She burst out in a forced laughing, then tried to restrain herself for fear that she might be overheard.
–Whit a temper he's got. He's like a wee boy, ken?
Ray shrugged, said –He's a redhead.
–Yeah. But he loves me really. I just like to wind him up a bit when he gets to taking me for granted
<pre>
                        which is all the time
                             so
                        they fight all the time?
</pre>
She lit a filter with a match
<pre>
                             but
                        consider the spaces
                          that are empty
                       but fill out the time
                         the coming down
                           forgiveness
                    perfect reunifying fucks
                    best parts of making up
                            No i Ray
                         these are two
                       i am a child to her
                          their child
                         the substitute
                            surrogate
                         the unaborted
</pre>
–Snap out o it, Ray.
–Eh?
–You're miles away.
–Just thinkin.
–That's no like you.
–Ha very good.
She got up, went to the mantlepiece. It was painted black, and only black, in a shiny finish gloss
<pre>
            and on it is a clock that is ticking loudly out
                the passing moments of our lives
                             now
                             now
                             now
</pre>
She is stubbing her cigarette, her back to Ray. She is momentarily the high priestess at the altar, bending down to switch off half the flameglow power
<pre>
                             now
                             now
                             now
</pre>

–Had a visit from the law.

She turns, converts her face to expression of annoyance, grimaces denoting the imparting of secret knowledge to the seeker who has come to her temple to consult her

> i ray set her free
> from her homerole
> now now

–Yeah? When?

–It was ok. Water running down from the ceiling in the flat below. They just wanted to check to see if it was coming from here. I took them in here, closed the door, went and hid the plants in the hall cupboard and then showed them round. But it was creepy, ken what I mean, the way they look, those uniforms. They try hard to be people but it's just not possible for them. The uniforms do that. Depersonalises them.

–Yeah. But then havent you got to have them, so people know.

–Maybe. Or maybe the uniform just gives them power in numbers, and makes us feel intimidated.

–But surely it's better to know. We dont want secret police do we?

–They cant be any thing other than secret, not unless everybody is one.

–Whit?

–A policer.

–Everybody? You mean like policing each other?

She shrugged, turned away.

–What secrets are secrets and which ones are open secrets. That's the point. Just how much do folk know.

She spoke like this was important, leaning towards him and pressing its significance by holding that position for a few seconds after the words had been spoken. Ray mulled it over in his mind, the words took on a deeper resonance, began association of numerous links which opened up the door for him to pry inside. Private lives and public knowledge.

Then Jan turned her head to show her profile. The swelling showed

> law near bust
> the scales and the weighing
> what is a guilty party
> and how do we determine it?

> the bruising and the blood-letting?
> the microscopic particles left behind?
> aye there's the victim
> with those wee bits of injustice on her cheek

–Like I know people know, and I dont mind that. I dont try to hide anything at all. I'm just me. Things go wrong sometimes, know what I mean? Living is a dying process, sure drugs are poisons, but so is sugar, so is salt. In fact they're all drugs, all foods. Everything we take into our bodies, right? It's to do with quantities, controlling intakes, maintaining the blood sugar iron nicotine levels. That way we control time, it's real time, the way we see it. Even the bad's necessary, things have got to be different. See with Joe and me, it's necessary for us to have our battles.

She turned and sat back down again. She looked away from him for quite some time, like she had said all she was going to say and the subject was completely off the table. Then she turned back to him again. The light from the window highlighted the bruising of her cheekbone which had still not gone from the week before

> martyr
> sacrificing
> knowledge
> for people she knows
> will abuse itwill I?
> would I?

She is woman susceptible but transcendent in everything she says and look, she gives, already in the next world waiting for her body to die

> o Ray

–Anyway I've got this place eh? Secure tenancy wi the council.

Jan's face was heavy with the weight of it all, she knew it could only be a matter of time till the clouds burst and the thunder man would come he would do it again or walk and then she'd be alone again, Ray knew she knew

> it might be tomorrow it might be today
> the day when you go and take your love away

–It's like ever since ma died, then the old man, this place has been mine, though they're still here, you know. It's good. You've no idea what a difference it makes. I'd had it wi rented rooms, bedsit land.

She looked about her at the room. The furniture had gone to the second hand shops a while ago, she didnt want it anyway, it wasnt her style all the Schreiber and Schreiber
                  oh
                  ii
                Ray
         say nothing now
            now now
              now
              now
But she had made it hers now
          and i respect that
   woman alone with men passing through
             taking
She crossed the room to the hifi and put a tape on.
             Bessie
              blue
             Bessie
              smith
          Smiths RIP
          Morrissey
    there's refuge in music
          from noise
–I went to church a week past Sunday. The cathedral down the west end.
  –Yeah?
           the church's
       better than nothing
Jan standing by the window, silhouetted. Slender frame, long hair, with the crisscross tree window frame a grid to measure her against. Tall ceiling
              con
         look up away
             ceiling
      secrets of the stone
        in the temple
–It was the first time in years, since my brother Frank got married. That was, letsee, 83. Weird. I just got up, decided to go and got dressed on impulse.
  Ray gestured towards the door.
          the absent one
         J for the red one
–Joe? Naw he stayed in bed.
      so that was the night it happened
        the bruise

A Day at the Office

Jan moved from the backlighting of the window, came to the couch, sat beside him. It was obvious now, the bloodshot red in the eye, the marks still there on her cheekbone from the week before.
—It's the drink Ray. Some folk cant handle it.
—The drink?
—Saturday you get drunk then Sunday you go to chapel.
everything to excess
primitive technique
She got up and went back to the window, having shown him how it was healing, having told him how she was healing it.
—It's quiet there. You dont have to think about God. You can just mediate.
mediate?
she means meditate
—Know what I mean? Tranquillity and you and there's nothing between you.
—Sure.
She moves quickly to her chair, from where she had begun
throwing
off the garbo
before she assumes it fully
now
now
skipping
air clear between them
tears unnecessary
—But I just wanted to, you know, remember what it was like. I used to go every week, you know, Sunday school, the lot.
—Me too
speaking of the which
Ray got up to go.
—You away?
—Aye, got to. I've got to try and sort out a couple of things. I just thought I'd nip in while I was up the dole.
—See you later then.
—Aye, see ya. I'll nip round tomorrow, see if the cheques come, get you that callydosh.
—Ok. Dont worry.
Ray smiled, sang – Be happy!

—That's the one.
—Right. He turned to the door. He went down the gloomy hall, opened the outside door and as he closed it, he heard them arguing with each other. It was drizzling as Ray came back down the hill to Tollcross. He had been walkabout and had a blister on his left heel, thanks to his two week old new second hand boots that were getting
>more fuckin painful by the step

The clocktower read
>timeless

Most of the shops were open and the pavement walkers were thinning out, though the street still buzzed with rush hour traffic.
>deli
>second hand washers
>hairdressers
>butchers advertising safe beef
>BSE free
>meek gents outfitter
>the Chinese Yellow hayfever takeaway
>did I think fever, say?
>here we are

He went into the Wayfarers café, having decided on his walk after a lot of penny counting that he could afford an egg roll and a cup of tea.
>not breakfast
>not luncheon
>brunchyawn
>people are wearing their butts
>off in offices
>in the buroo
>mule

Freddie was on the stool by the till as usual, watching the black and white portable. He was a sports fanatic, as far as watching it went. Along with his mother, he ran the place. She was a strange old biddy, hardly spoke a word of English though she'd left Italy as a wee lass. She did the main meals, lasagne and chips, that kind of thing and Fred took care of the teas and coffees, the hot snacks and the icecreams
>and the money

The place hadnt changed since Ray could remember, since the times he used to come in with his ma when they were up the toon, though it had been painted out now and again, it was

A Day at the Office

always the same combination of browns and orange. Probably didnt show the nicotine stains. The only concession to modern times was the microwave. But it was cheap and Freddie was easygoing. He seemed to like Ray. They talked about the football mainly. Ray had been a big fan as a boy and he still kept up with the back page news from time to time. Freddie knew everything there was to know and not just about the football, though that was his main interest – behind the counter, now spotted with grease from the chip vat, was a team photo of the Italian World Cup winning side of 82.

– It looks like you're gonnæ have another to keep it company in a few months. Home team and that.

–You better believe it.
> faith's not a lost thingy
> all I can say
> is

–Gotta be a good bet.

–Aye. Sure thing, I reckon. Seen this Vialli? Freddie breathes, rounding his lips, whew! what a player
> good fitba joy to the ee

–So where you been today then? Signing on day is it?

Freddie is the adept at sizzling the egg on the hotplate, slow careful hand, never fails to keep it just right.
> kind face
> balding
> black hair when it was
> not old yet
> but fat
> off the land

–Yeah.

–You never think of getting a job, Ray? Get some cash together, get away.

Ray shrugs.
> think of it?
> when do I stop?

–Young guy like you, no strings. What makes you hang around here, eh?

–You got a girl up your sleeve or something?

–Not exactly.

–I mean come on, look at this place, dont you want to see a bit of sun?

–Who needs the sun wi a name like mine? Anyway I love

January in Scotland. The long faces, the bitter wind. It's good for the spirit.
                    who are you kiddin
                       chum
   –Oh aye, very true! You want sauce?
   –Sauce and salt.

1000

my heart is ticking
like a telex
but here in the office
the condition of an organ
is of little concern
to the corporate good
which sways upon the shoulder
of the overseer's leer
it sniffs
CURE YOURSELVES AND SO SECURE
TOMORROW
in this renewal
you must choose
new versions of your names
and signatures
TRY
a new diet
SPORT
a new haircut
FIND
a new lover
DANCE
at the office party
but oh the dance is always so
dull
the same plod slowstep
round the floor
the same bandmaster
and the partner
is always as old as your mother
tell me
where is the man in his car
driving in the adverts to
is he driving home
or will he visit the empress
Douglas knows

As he pulls up in front of the house, he sees that his mother's Volvo isnt there and remembers that she has changed her golf morning. He lets himself in the back door, turning the key

which she has made him keep – not that he hadnt wanted it, only the symbolic significance had made him offer it all. He is glad to have it, even though the house isnt home anymore. Here in the tree-lined cul-de-sac, away from the hustle of the city centre, the tranquil air is familiar and pleasant. As is this house, the place where he spent so much time, where a complete life has been lived
already
to death
But he took all he wanted when he left. His mother keeps his room much as it was and sometimes he stays the night, but that is a rare occurrence, and he does it for her sake, really, because she is lonely here. But it isnt home now, it is a naggingly beautiful old house, though
the old house
where the violin played
can never be remade.
 She is lonely, though she tries not to let him see. Under the superfice of the busy suburban lady she appears to be, playing golf and entertaining, active in local charities and all that, she is lonely. He had been the last to leave, a grown man of twenty-six when he finally did, kept there by his understanding of the vacuum he would gift her when he left, though in the end, she had almost seemed to want him gone, as if she had become perplexed by his reluctance to take an interest in the outside world. But now all that was past. He could call in, check on her and leave without that sense of tension interloping between them
and our difference
He decides to make himself some of her peppermint tea. From the cupboard above the electric kettle, he takes out a cup which has emblazoned upon it the 'family crest' as she is wont to call it. Though she now spoke in an ironic manner when she mentioned it, this emblem has always been an affectation he has felt uncomfortable about, to the extent of being ashamed of her behaviour at dinner parties he was forced to attend in his early teens. It nevertheless intrigues him
as a metaphor for her place
in my life
The design is her own handiwork from many years before, consisting of a shield with a silver eagle on a purple

background, the emblem of the sublimated soul in the bosom of spirituality. The dinner set bearing this legend which she commissioned some twenty years earlier has long since ceased to be current. Pieces were broken, chipped and what remained intact was retired gracefully from display and dinner party use, to form a functional part of everyday life, gradually receding in abundance as the years passed
till now
only odd bits remain
Imagining her as she was then, huge and centrally placed in his child world, infallible and not to be questioned at length, he remembers a young smiling woman with beautiful auburn hair, kissing him and tucking his vest in, encouraging him to work hard, tidy up his room and say thank you. Enthusiastic about her home and family to outsiders, who included her own relations. He could not entirely forget that the whole hustling circus she now looked down on was the world in which she herself grew up. The tenemented streetfront gardenless dementia squashed between the crags and the river, at the bottom of the long lowgraded slope up from the river bank to the shoulder of the mounthill, this had been her world as a child, and she had known it from the inside
with
the voice of Them
in her head
He had seen the photographic evidence at his grandmother's flat, though it disappeared after grandmother died. Proud but poor people living in an environment they felt superior to, giving themselves to an only daughter reared to succeed and get out, while she tried to balance their demands on her with those of her schoolmates. The power of her parents' determination finally won through. She was the future, the generation for whom they had fought the war
that precious pearl
Our Frances
The arrangement of space and things has not changed in the kitchen. Everything has been taken care off, perhaps enhanced by additional detail as time has passed. The morning light streams through the little east-facing window with the stained glass fleur-de-lis peak as it has always done. The wall on which that light falls still plays hostess to that silhouetted

pattern. The begonias and geraniums that she has tended year by year thrive as always in the south window behind the sink, perhaps cuttings of cuttings of cuttings of the original plants, but indistinguishable from them to his eye. Perpetuation of the line through history has been her aim.

He hears the car outside in the drive. The engine slows and stops,
putters
to silence
The car door shuts. A key turns click in the lock. She comes in swinging a couple of carrier bags, pushing the door open with her shoulder.

«Well hello. I thought you were in London,» she says setting the bags on the unit top behind the door.

«Just back,» he answers. «I came up overnight to avoid the worst of the traffic.»

She crosses to where he sits and pecks him on the cheek with lip-sticked lips. She examines him at close range, her face stiff. He sees the carefully disguised lines that parallel the many trenches she has dug to hold her position while the enemy, age, attacks
crisscross
kiss
kiss
«Douglas, you look very pale, dear. Why dont you stay and have some lunch with me ?»

He shakes his head. She is drawing him in sweetly,
syrup sucking
lick the spoon
little man?
«No really, I cant. I have people to see today. I just thought I'd drop in as I passed. I forgot you'd changed your golfing day.»
stick to schedule
He peers into the small mirror which hangs from the wooden surround of the window above the kitchen sink, while she begins unpacking her shopping. He sees that she is right, that he does look run down. Under his eyes are half moons of alarmingly grey colouring where the soft flesh has no support from the bone of his cheek. His hair is without shine and his skin appears plastic and dead. He pulls at the grey moon

below his right eye and examines the part of the eye which is covered by the skin

internal red
pulsing still

«I drove up overnight,» he explains to himself, to her, to neglected health, as he turns away from the mirror. «Once I've finished what I've got to do, I'll have a good night's sleep and that'll cure it.»

She is unloading a bag of fresh fruit and vegetables. Grapes, soft peaches off season, apples, carrots, onions, and potatoes in the bottom of the bag, all packaged by the hand of the best greengrocer in the area.

«You could go and have a nap in your room if you like. It would only take a moment to air the ... »

«Ma it's not my room now.»

«Well you know where I mean, don't you? It's not as if you've forgotten, have you?» She gives no hint of annoyance in her face, the same bland fullness of warmth is there to be seen, though he knows that

irked
she does not bite
but purrs fiercely

her dignity sustains her. The old room is unchanged, awaiting him, but will not come to seek him out.

«Well how about dinner tonight instead? Hilda and Barbara are coming round.»

«Barbara? Is she here?»

«Yes. She arrived yesterday, I think.»

«How long is she staying?»

«I'm not sure dear.»

The carrier bag is neatly folded without hurry and placed in the drawer reserved for carrier bags. She reuses them, carries only those displaying the names of companies she approves of. So Harrods and House of Fraser convey her purchases wherever she shops. He watches, thinking of Barbara, his surrogate sister, now resident in Florida, a woman he perhaps loves but cannot bring himself to like although he truly wants to

satisfy my curiosity
compare
the two of us
and what we have become

since that last time.
«Will you come?»
«I dont know. I'd like to see her, but ... »
«Please, Douglas dear, it would be so nice to have the two of you here together. Like old times, you know. Hilda and I and our two children.»

Her smile is a magnet and he an iron filing. He is scanning quickly through the journey he has plotted in his mind for the day, checking its planning to see where time could be saved or shortcuts made. Perhaps to do this now may buy time later, and tired as he is from the driving, he is more than ready to be persuaded.

«Yes I will,» he decides, nodding, «I'd like to see her. If I could leave one or two things here, till tomorrow, I should be able to get free by about seven or eight. How does that sound?»

«Super, we can eat at nine,» his mother answers, as she picks up three tins and stacks them in the bottom of the fridge. «You know you're welcome to whatever you need, darling.»

«Still keeping everything in there are you?» he grins. It had been a family joke, her attachment to the chiller as a storehouse. But now only they comprise the family. She smiles, the allusion understood.

«Helps keep things fresh, dear.» They chuckle in harmony, the same rhythmic laugh,
<pre>
           a sound that reaffirms our closeness
                       a bond
                        that
                   has its origins in
                 the music of her womb
                         its
                       lullaby
                      laughter
                   gurgling boomble
</pre>
«Can I make you a drink? Coffee?»

He holds up his empty cup for her to see.

«I helped myself to your peppermint tea.»

But he is now committed to the serving of her wishes, to carrying her sceptre. The family crest weaves them into one threaded story. He is her child and there can be no refutation of this reality. She it is, and only she that binds him to mortality at all

> when I would rather fly
> die
> of loneliness

She it is that keeps him from leaving his self without a name. She who reminds all the time that he is Shaw, Douglas Shaw and that the Shaws were something in this city once. The first wee shoppe in Atholl Street, great grandfather the country boy come in t'toon and henceforth making for himself a place to put his name above the door of:

> *JAMES SHAW (Merchant)*

And then the children growing: the professorial one, the property developer, the genial drinker and raconteur. And the children's children growing as

> the academic
> the artist
> the lawyer
> the soldier
> the seaman
> and the drinker

The gene of the drinker recurred again in his father, though he was soldier, business man and drinker all combined. And Scots to the last man, says the rugby cap of grand uncle George.

The vanity of it all is seductive. He could allow himself to be drawn into it without even having a second glance at the outside world and the way in which it is different from the world that he, when within this family heritage, inhabits.

Yet there were other bits of it that were not spoken of. Ungloried failures and malfunctions of the machine that was the lineage. His own father who divorced his first wife because she had not borne an heir, though like the Empress Josephine, she was still in attendance as his cancerous end approached, and would have gone to him had she been allowed. And Hugh his elder brother, who melted down by the time he was thirty-five, who could overlook the sense of failure that remained the single biggest shareholder in their memories of him.

The Campbell's soup tin lady, as they used to call her, as children whispering underneath the bed, could not have predicted such an outcome, and despite her fierce defiance of the facts as they presented themselves to her in the form of the wasting Hugh, she could cry a lot if she had a mind to once begin. Her scorn, of what she herself once was, did not run so far as to make her hard or callous to the suffering of her immediate family.

«Go on, have a coffee with me, it'd be so nice.»

«Oh Ma, you'll make me late.»

«What could be more important than spending time with me?»

Her tone is the family crest tone, a self reverential centring after a rise

                     and I cant leave
                        the court
               of she who rules here

1035
in life
as in
coffee breaks
more tales of failure
reach an ashtray grave
than of achievement
we must talk
HIGHER FASTER
deeper closer
never stop this chatter
*become the moving dead
each night
ah
to be rising only now
slowly
pausing over details
to be with Helen*

in her kitchen, as she puts her espresso pot on the gas and sits down at the table to wait for it to bubble. The room is damp and cold and the window begins to mist over with condensation as the temperature rises

damp

The smell of gas tinges the air, while outside the grey sky has cleared slightly and it is possible that the sun might break through the cloud. Above the tenement block which backs onto this one, a kind of silver starfish shape is appearing in the gloomy covering, which marks the point in the heavens that the sun has reached in its shallow winter arc. The ash tree that grows in the centre of the back green is swaying branches in the gusting wind. The events of the morning resonate in her mind as the siren that woke her rings in her ears. The visit of the policemen and her involvement in their procedures has woven her into the life of the street.

As she rises from her chair to switch the flame off, little sizzling dark brown spits escape from the worn gasket of the pot. The pungent aroma of burning coffee slowly filling the room sparks her sleepy head to thought.

make it sweet
for energy
for effect

She wonders just how many times has she spoken to old Mrs King, half a dozen maybe? Certainly it could be little more than that. An average of less than one exchange every month since she moved in, and not even exchanges, just collisions over the washing line in the back green, or on the pavement on the streetside. Yet Mrs King is one of the prominent characters of Foundry Lane, and she knows the woman's herstory quite intimately. She has heard her talking in her croaky voice to the young mum who lives below her, in the summer when the weather was warm and she had the kitchen window open. Conversations between them were generally one sided, the old woman commenting on the goings on of her peculiar world, or telling an assortment of tales, as her neighbour, pegs in her mouth, hung out the nappies, responding with the occasional 'is that right?', 'oh?', and her favourite 'really?' She has listened not to eavesdrop so much as to become familiar with the place and its people. The old heart of the city where she now lives was alien to her even though she had spent her whole life living on the fringes of it. It was a place that she had come to for schooling, for shopping, for dancing, but never one she had lived in. Until now.

Mrs King's story is of a girl who came from the islands to work as a maid in a townhouse, who fell pregnant to an apprentice tanner and lived most of her married life in awful poverty, till her kids grew up and left home. But by then she was too old and tired to appreciate the extra space and cash, and the ease it brought. Her husband died, still quite a young man, of lung cancer. Her ten kids hardly ever come to see her. Most of them have moved far away, to America or was it Australia, to England.

Now she has her three he-cats for company, one of them a giant white that was always wandering off. Sometimes you would hear her, stumbling about among the bushes and the weeds that tangle round the rusty metal railings in the wasteground behind the washing lines, calling its name: 'Bambi?'

<pre>
          rustle
          twigsnap
          'Bambi?'
          bambino
          baby
</pre>

A Day at the Office

And she had a liking for a drink or two, judging by appearances. Helen had seen her buying her half bottle of whisky in the off licence on the corner. Sometimes she seemed to go a bit loopy with it, like her memory was failing her now
stretched
too thinly between past and present
will only snap back
connecting
0
with
0
where was she then¿

The first Helen knew of the incident was the siren and the carry-on in the street outside, the ambulance and then the sound of agitated voices talking. The noise had woken her up. When she pulled up the sash and stuck her head out to see what was going on, a man hanging out the window of the flat next to hers told her that Mrs King had been found unconscious by the home help, with a bloody great bruise on her forehead.
life happens to you like this
takes you inside
like it or not
She had explained this to the first policeman, and he had listened, nodding intermittently while waiting a chance to interject that yes, of course he understood, but still they must investigate fully. This had been a serious assault. He had asked her name and in saying the sounds *Hel-en-Orr*, in telling him that she had come home from work in the early hours of the morning, and saw the lights on in Mrs King's, she became a link in the unfolding of the callous assault in Foundry Lane between the hours of twelve midnight and nine-thirty am.

She had answered his questions carefully, not wanting to appear as if she was concealing anything, while giving away the least possible information about herself. But it was clear he wanted more from her. If it was convenient, another officer would call later in the morning to take a full statement, and yes, nodding she would like to help in any way she can but if she had anything to tell she would have come forward, and yes, nodding, he understood that, but nevertheless, shall we say around eleven? She agreed just to get him out of the flat.

Now she wonders will the kids come? All consumed with guilt for having neglected their duties? Not that she cares, she cant afford to. Because it could just be that old Mrs King had got drunk, then fallen and bashed her head in. And what if it had been a mugging? What difference would that make, really? What could she Hel-en do about it?

> it's not as if it was
> something that I
> can influence

She cant afford to care. There are too many pitiable people about, all waiting for the slightest sign of sympathy, so they can grip on to you

> like a leech sucking into a fresh supply
> With a leech you can burn it off
> but with a person it's different
> you can feel their agony
> like it was your own

This old woman had withered away, sucked of life by her kids, a bundle of bones in an old dry skin. She was the victim, not suddenly because of this incident, but because of the being of the rejected Mother

> Oh they might come now
> now that she was broken
> they might even cry
> but what good would that do?
> twas the way it was.

Guilt was the problem, the thing to be avoided. The erosion of wholeness by regret. Helen-O is careful not to care, because in caring she is drawn too deeply in and begins to feel the pain and suffer with the suffering. She cant allow herself to think of how Colin may be feeling now that she has left him, for then she will begin to remember the promises her nineteen year-old self made to him about true love and everlasting togetherness and how he still believes that, because it suits him to believe it and if he can convince her then it will go on the way that it has been before, for four suffocating years. She must shut it out and concentrate on

> me
> now

She drinks her coffee in sips and puts another image in her mind. There is the crematorium up the road with that keen air of silence, and this will have the last ounce of warmth out of all the Mrs Kings. And Helen Orr is not going to be cracked

again. She isnt going to allow it. She is coolly awake
<pre>
         Mother has never been other
                        in
                the dread of the night
                       but
                the need to be right
</pre>
She fills her cup from the pot of coffee. Some drops spill into the blue rimmed saucer. Looking out the window to the back green, where Mrs King had crawled about the bushes looking for Bambi she sees once again for the n-teenth time that the old ash tree is completely stripped of leaves.

The second policeman arrived about eleven. He introduced himself as David Simpson CID. His tall solid figure seemed to fill the door of the flat. She looked into his face and saw a boychild under the beard, read his fiery temper and his egotist essence. He was wearing a short black leather jacket, neat cut striped shirt and black police issue trousers, his face and the way he announced himself seemed to say that he was no ordinary man but
<pre>
                       el cid
                 a man of mystery
                 secrets concealed
                  in every skinfold
</pre>
though to her eye he was covering nothing of himself in glory but was naked sitting there, his emperor's new clothes threadbare transparent, saying far too much about him while
<pre>
                      I want
                   to be opaque
                 outwardly tuneless
                  bland not exotic
          not clad in metal or the hide of animals
</pre>
He asked if he could hear her story. She took him into the bedsitting room, where he immediately began scanning round the place.

'Quite a reader, eh?' he observed, then turned and sat down uninvited. His bulk filled the small gold couch, and as he took out his notebook it was clear that he was waiting, not for dictation but for revelation.
<pre>
             a figure seated on a throne
                   a cube of gold
</pre>
He smiled at her, it was a leering look, overly familiar
<pre>
                     a prelude
</pre>

> vaulting formality
> into intimacy

His presence was not wanted. He had no business to be there. The creaking squeaking of his jacket grated on her nerves, but she had to sit and face him. He was to begin asking the questions by going over things that she had already told the first policeman, so reminding her that she was already part of the process.

'Now then, your name is Helen Stanton Orr?'
'Yes.'

> yes yes
> you know that

'You came home at three-thirty last night?'
'About then.'

> what's the diff?

'And can I have the name and address of the premises where you work?'
'The Berkeley Casino, in Kinnoull Street.'
'The Berkeley?' He raised his eyebrows. 'What exactly do you do there?'

> above him is a black eagle
> and the Force is behind

'I'm just a waitress in the restaurant on the ground floor.'
He grinned, regal in his role in control.
'Gambling really fascinates me,' he said, leaning back, screwing his eyes so she could hardly see into them.
'I never went up to the casino. I refused a job as a croupier.'
'Did you really? Would it not be better money?'
'Yes but that's not the point. I dont want to work there forever. I dont want to make a career of it.'

> money is never better
> at all
> ever
> only distilled time
> who wants to save it up for old age
> when one might break before

'Yes, gambling fascinates me, you know,' he repeated. 'Not that I play the tables so much myself, it's more that I like to watch the kind of characters that go there. I mean I have a wee flutter, but ... '
he

> laughs a slow knowing sound

A Day at the Office

gave her that look of intimacy again. 'Money's not so easy to come by.'

Helen tried to give no response, she tried to make her facial expression and her stance say leave me alone, but he had a certain power, a definite threatening power that seemed to lie in the fact that he was on the side of the law and therefore considered himself and his motives above suspicion.

'But it's fascinating. It's the sight of people's will crumbling, right? The different ways they show it.'

He gave a glance that seemed to suggest that whether she would admit it or not, he was onto something here, some deep psychological angle on the business he was examining.

'Only the Chinese seem able to hide it. If they feel it at all, that is. Have you noticed that?

> in his hand he holds
> the globe of the world
> believes it to be
> the world

Though she wanted to speak out, to tell him that she had refused the job as a croupier because of the very sight that he found so intriguing, she didnt. There was something about his manner that seemed to forbid her from taking the situation lightly, from speaking out and so giving something of herself away to him. She felt that he was wandering from his business, forming an image of her in his mind that was mistaken, and that she resented. He seemed to be looking her over with the eye of a man who believes himself to be a connoisseur of women, a man who has a harem at his beckon

> people never look at people
> without assuming that they know
> of someone who is like them

She knew the look well. It was something she had come across many times before. Something in her teens that she had welcomed as a positive response to how she dressed. But now, here in her home, it felt like a subtle kind of rape. The slick, well-oiled professional tongue was flicking over her ears, poking in and out of her private life space. The old woman's assault had become the instrument of another kind of assault and Helen felt herself prepare to recoil into monosyllabic replies and dismissive gestures. She thought

> he thinks he is
> the image of Hercules

> holding his club
> the golden apples he has taken
> from the garden of the Hesperides

He fingered the paper on which only a few marks have been made. The activation of his programming is just this white space.

'Did you see anything suspicious at all?'

'Like what?' she asked

> that he has me under his thumb

'Anyone hanging around outside?'

'No. I took a taxi. He dropped me off at the main door. I was tired, I just opened the door and went in.'

'Did you happen to notice if there were any lights on in the flat concerned?'

'I cant be sure but I think so.' Again something seemed to force her subjection, into offering more than she really wanted to. 'She drinks, you know.'

He raised his eyebrows. 'You think she was drinking last night?' The way in which the question was phrased was like a quizmaster on tv who's got the answer on the card in front of him.

'I dont know.'

He put away his notebook. She had tried to deflect the questioning by a lack of response.

And it wasnt until he had suggested that he might see her there sometime, off-duty of course, that he finally stood up to leave. But still she didnt deny the possibility. She just bit her tongue and moved him towards the door slowly. He turned and gave her a half wink as he started down the stair.

1117

it's the same old same old
freedom's such a sacrifice
of
say MONEY *it*
STATUS
who i am

who am I
more
than
THIS
neck tie
more wise
than any skin bone sage
THAN ANY OLD FRIEND
CLAIMING YOUVE BETRAYED
SOME TREASURED SECRET
i'll stay a while at this
the pay's not bad
and i'm so hungry
i could eat a horse
so long as it's meat
and bloody
TOGETHER
WE COULD GO FAR
ME
HERE BEHIND
YOU
IN THERE WORKING
WITH THE SCHEDULE
LAID OUT
ON MY
MASTER PLANNER
yet still i'd rather be

speeding on the dual carriageway along the riverside, through acres of suburban bungalows and semis free, he soon crossed the city boundary and reached the low, flat farmland on the estuary banks. The sensation of power arising from the driving encouraged an expansive beam to cover his face. The choices represented to him by the various signposts reminded him that he was free to go where he wanted. But, knowing this, he felt no urge to deviate from the journey already plotted in his mind.

> it's so hard to really know this
> that the flower of zen
> is in my hand and floats
> with me in this machine

Manipulation of the controls was easy, their sure, unfaltering response comforting. It seemed that no obstacle could exist to his forward motion, that every goal was attainable with persistence. The concert of Schubert's Lieder on the radio did not affect his mood with its melancholy, but simply tinted everything with an extra dimension of beauty. Across the wide river mouth, the faint blue peaks of northern mountains formed a rolling wavelike pattern. Beyond this was the empty land, the moors lying dormant in a cold wide moonscape. He would not go there

> but by the shady water flow
> a child of nature
> ULP
> drop down
> pull out
> hit the floor
> fourth
> cruise past

Reaching the turnoff to Stuart's cottage, he slowed the car, to travel the last two miles down to the shoreline over the uneven road. Through a screen of winter trees, he saw the house, a small, white dot on the beach head, clear against the grey sea. This place was beautiful. A haven, warm and welcoming at the end of the drive. It was more than Stuart deserved.

He was in the greenhouse built onto the side of the cottage, where he was daubing the wooden frame with white paint, standing on top of a chair dressed in an old boilersuit. He didnt see Douglas coming and looked up in surprise when he opened the door and stuck his head inside.

«Busy?»

Stuart shook his head. «Potterin.» He balanced the paintbrush across the top of the can and climbed down from the

A Day at the Office

chair. «So what brings you out here then?»

Douglas smiled. «I've come to sing you Happy Birthday.»

«For chrissakes dont remind me,» Stuart scowled. «I'm dying with the flu or something and here you are reminding me I'm now in the depths of middle age – though if I can realistically expect to live to be eighty, after my career of debauchery, is seriously doubtful.»

touched nerve
we two
never really
not bristling

Entering through the back kitchen, they went into the living end of the cottage. A recently built log fire was smouldering in the grate and, as always, the place was a mess of books, cold cups and newspapers. Douglas had to move a scrappy old Penguin Buddhist Scriptures before he could sit down. Stuart took off his working boots, stripped off his overalls and kicked them into a corner in a crumpled heap. He knelt down to inspect the unhappy fire. After a minute prodding with a poker, he stood up.

avoid it
this attack

«It'll take,» he muttered to himself, then turned to Douglas, smiled and sat down on an armchair by the fireside. Douglas produced the little snuffbox he had brought and handed it over to Stuart. Stuart opened it and poked at the halfgram of coke inside.

«Happy birthday,» Douglas said.

Stuart's expression was strangely uncertain. «Thought you were going to sing it,» he muttered.

«You know, it's a long time since I had a smoke even,» he said quietly. «I've been living the straight life since you last saw me, working hard.» He looked again at the box.

«This is just going to spoil me, you know. I wont be able to get a thing done.»

With a chuckle, Douglas said «We're all going on soma holiday», in a half singing voice. «Remember?»

Stuart laughed. «I suppose I was as big a prick then as you are right now,» he said. «But more important, have you got time for a game? That's what I really need. The real problem with my new found independence in isolation is not having

anybody to play Go with.»
>>>
seeing in those hands
the memory
first initiation into drug culture
stoned for the first time.
>>>
And brother Hugh is dead now, though somehow present, defined by the space between them. Stuart more than anyone had helped him through it. He had helped him out
>>>
out of the sheltered world
in his mother's pocket
>>>
After his brother died. He was grateful for that.

«You seem very quiet today, troubles?»

Douglas laughed. «No. Just the opposite in fact.»

He passed the j he had been smoking in the car.

«Oh?»

«So what is it that's had such a calming effect on your tongue?»

«Well ... » he hesitated. «Come on, out with it.» Stuart got up and went through to the back kitchen where he filled the electric kettle.

«I dont know how to put it,» Douglas began. «I mean it's not so hard to say, it's just that it's ... well it's Helen.»

At first there was no sound from the kitchen. Then Stuart appeared in the doorway, looking stunned. «Helen?» he said, «You mean, you and Helen?» His face was strangely blank. Douglas felt, all of a sudden, boyish and silly, like he was confessing his first affair of the heart to his mother
>>>
it's
it's
she
>>>
He could only nod in affirmation. Stuart scratched his head. «Well well. You and my wee sister!» He turned away into the kitchen again
>>>
stiff lip
hides a snarl
>>>
Douglas was irritated by his lack of positive reaction.

«It's not so unlikely, is it? It was you that suggested she should take the flat.»

Stuart came out carrying the teapot and two mugs. His face looked oddly unhappy.

«I wasnt matchmaking, if that's what you're saying,» he muttered, putting the pot on the tiled fireplace.

«I dont know. It just seems like..» he hesitated, «Like ... well I've always thought of you as a wee brother. Especially since Hugh died, you know. It's like it was incestuous or something ... .» Then he smiled. «But that's daft, isnt it?»
       not daft
      bitter perhaps
Stuart brought out the Go board and the stones, placed it between them in front of the fire. He picked a stone out of each bowl, shook them together in cupped hands and held his closed fists out for Douglas to choose
        left hand
A white stone in his palm
      so it's black for me
Stuart made his first play to the corner at Douglas' right hand. Douglas made a corresponding move
     meet me at the corner
«I get the impression you're not altogether happy about Helen and me,» he said, as the stone clicked into position.
  «Ach, Dougie man. It's not that,» he said, making another territorial marker on a vacant corner. «It's just that Helen's been through a lot for somebody her age. When you said about the flat being empty, I thought it would be good for her to try being independent for a while. Not get into another relationship right away, know what I mean?» The stones were rapidly drawing the shape of the game.
  «She's always been the baby of the family,» Stuart went on. «Protected. When she married that Colin, she was only seventeen. It was just straight out of one cosy nest and into another. But he was such a shit, man, you've no idea. Used to knock her about.»
      big brother onto you
      give you the doing
      you deserve
He was talking and playing without looking at Douglas.
  «The thing is, I'm just worried she might be looking to you to replace him or the family, when she should really be standing on her own feet for a change. She's got so much potential, know what I mean? The things she thinks up, man. She's really sharp.»
  The first few moves had left black with a slight territorial advantage. But it was white's play and Douglas attacked,

placing the stone inside the sketched black corner, threatening a clean division of space along the diagonal
>fold the square
>into triangles two

«I dont think that's what's happening, Stuart. I'm not trying to say I know her better than you, but she's changed since she moved in.» Stuart reacted to the spatial threat by placing a second strong stone alongside his first, creating an obstacle to Douglas' attack
>flick back
>nothing dictated
>free stone
>rolling

«The thing is, Dougie, I dont know her. She was only a kid when I moved down to London. It's only since I moved back up here that I've gotten to know her. Over the last couple of years, really. But I cant help feeling that she hasnt had a proper run at it yet. Like there's always been somebody else there, blocking her. Maybe because they love her and want to help her.»
>means me
>obviously

He glanced over at Douglas, who was studying the board, considering his next move. The attack he had begun hinged upon its positioning. It was a very difficult decision. If he pressed for the corner, he ran the risk of being cut off, surrounded and captured. He hesitated, looked away, then studied it afresh. He tried to recall the advice Stuart had given him years before, when he was learning the game
>look at it from your opponent's point of view
>deduce his next move

Finally he played safe, extending his formation along the edge of the board, away from the corner
>next of value
>next of kin

Stuart immediately confirmed his advantage with a consolidating play.

«Did you ever read Brautigan's book, *The Abortion*?», he asked
>shake head

«There's this character in it, a woman who feels like she has been born into the wrong body, because it's so beautiful and attracts people to her, though she doesnt feel beautiful inside

A Day at the Office

at all. I think it's that one. Do you know it?»
referring of course
to she
does he
want her?

Douglas shook his head. Stuart was waiting for his play, but Douglas wanted time to think about it, to look at the whole board as it was developing. To get drawn into one small area of it was foolish. He felt as if Stuart was holding something back from him, some scheme that he'd worked out.

«It may be dated now, the style and that, very sixties. But that kind of thing, where a person gets lost inside their own body, when they come to see their inside and their outside like they're in conflict with each other, it's really self-destructive. The alienation of the private self from the public. That kind of thing.»
that thing you speak of
is

Suddenly Douglas saw the move. If he didnt build space now, Stuart could force his formation out into the centre of the board where it would be in real trouble. He played the stone that gave him width
broader than a line
three points
make three lines

Stuart nodded gently, six or seven times.

«Very good. I can see you've been thinking about it.»

Now it was him that had the puzzle
take that varlet
I
have at you
thrust

«I understand what it is you're saying, Stuart,» sticking the papers together.

«Helen's got that air of tension about her. But it isnt just her body that makes her beautiful. It's also that very air of tension that you're describing. The fact that she isnt fully aware of herself, like ... like..»
what is it I mean
why wont the image come?

He couldnt think of a suitable simile.

Stuart was nodding in agreement.

«I know, I know what you mean.»

>how can you when I didnt say it?

«But it's very vulnerable, that state of mind.»

He laughed gently, taking the smoke from Douglas.

«Maybe I'm being overprotective myself, I dont know. Maybe I'm guilty of caring too.»

>what's that?
>caring
>guilty

As he played the attacking stone into the white corner, their stances reversed

>switch back
>blade
>sharpen it

«That's the wrong word,» Douglas said quickly. «You cant be guilty of caring.»

He placed his white defensive move right next to Stuart's attacking stone. The speed of Stuart's response told him he had made an error.

«Damn!»

>damn damn

Stuart laughed again.

«Guilty of caring? Oh I think we can. I think that caring can be the most destructive force there is, because it can blind you, totally, to the truth. Or the need for some kind of rational outlook.»

>love is blinded
>damn u

His voice had a finality about it, and although Douglas wasnt satisfied with Stuart's answer, he didnt challenge him. The board was filling, reaching beyond mid-game now. It was hard to make any prediction about the outcome. Black had a slight advantage, with half of a white corner following the last exchange, but it wasnt much

>more than a promise

Douglas studied the board for a while silently and after a few moments, he spotted what looked like a weakness in the black formation on the left edge of the board. A chance to take five, maybe six stones, as he played the vital point, uttering the warning of attack

«Hatari!»

>hatari

Stuart's jerky response told him he had not anticipated the danger

A Day at the Office

too late now

Douglas leaned back from the board, feeling pleased with himself. Stuart stared at the problem for a while, then relaxed from the play. He rolled a cigarette and glanced at Douglas, who couldnt hide his satisfaction.

quits
quite

«No need to look so smug about it,» Stuart said as he stood up. «Time for coffee, I think. My brain needs a little stimulus. I'm not used to smoking like this.»

He went through to the kitchen again. The coffee-making ritual began. First the slow roasting of the beans in the grill. Then the cooling and the grinding, the precise wait as the hot water fused with the minute particles of flavour. Douglas admired his patience, his single-mindedness, intent on doing the thing as well as possible. Hugh had been like that too, where coffee and Go were concerned, before he got into smack. It was something Stuart and him had got into together

like so much
like Art school
the whole hippy happy trail
like the drug thing

But Stuart had survived. It was Hugh they had buried. The one who had the real ability. Stuart was here now, back where he had started from, older and wiser, still painting

his sloppy abstracts
selling nothing

somehow surviving. Where did the money come from? He had started out with nothing, a kid from one of the estates, and he'd never made it as a painter.

«Deep thought?»

Douglas looked up. Stuart was standing in the doorway, holding a tray with the Meito china coffee set that Douglas had given to his brother the year before he died. Everything was so mixed up. Like a tangled game of Go, where black and white formations were so interlinked and cut so often that lines were indistinguishable, where nothing made sense.

«It's nothing,» Douglas lied. «Just stoned.»

Stuart brought the coffee to the game.

«You still dealing then?» Stuart asked, as he put the tray down.

«Some.»

«You should get out of it, Douglas. It's a messy business, and it's going to get worse. Years ago, it was different. There wasnt the same opposition. Now you get five years for an ounce.»

He poured the coffee carefully and handed a cup to Douglas
>   with a kindly smile
>   squash the beetle
>   that is scarab
>   in my life

Douglas shrugged, but he was annoyed.

«It's just a sideline. Once I've got the gallery underway, I wont have time for it any longer.»

Stuart glanced at him as he sipped from his cup. «Take my advice,» he said «Better knock it on the head now. It's not worth the risks anymore. I dont want to sound like some old fogey, you know. But it's true, Douglas. I like you. I feel responsible in a way. Hugh and me, well we were real close, you know that. I've learnt a lot since then. You just cant play around with these things. They're poisons. I dont just mean smack, man. It's the whole business, the people you get mixed up with. It's changed now.»

>   all change
>   I did it and you cant
>   even though

Douglas said nothing. He turned back to the unfinished game. Stuart joined him. A quick succession of moves led them into the confrontation of the centre board. Here Douglas found his formation cut in two places and knew that some sacrifice had to be made. He lost seven stones and with them went the game. The remainder of the moves were of little importance to the outcome, consisting of little more than merely filling in the holes. In the count, black won by thirteen. Stuart leaned back and smiled. Douglas was annoyed at him. It was as if, even when Douglas had surprised him with his small gain in the mid-game, he had always believed that the victory would ultimately be his

>   that the game was his
>   the drug was his
>   the world was his
>   my brother was his

Stuart was turning the gift over in his right palm with the fingers of his left hand, slowly, considering.

A Day at the Office

«Douglas, I dont want you thinkin ... » He hesitated, then sighed. «Look at it this way, I want to get away from all this. I'm tryin to do without it.» He held the little box up between finger and thumb

reject
deject

«I mean I know what you want, I think I do, kid. But I'm not him, Hugh I mean, I'm not even the Stuart you knew then. I'm not trying to say that you shouldnt come, but don't try and involve me, I dont want it. I dont want this.»

He handed the gift back.

«And I ... Helen ... Dont do anything to screw her up, she's had enough. Just give her space to grow, man, that's all.»

space
my space
is mine

«Understand?»

Douglas shrugged and moved his head in a vague way that transmitted neither nod nor shake.

«Come, I'm not saying dont come, just let it be because you want to, not because of him, or her, or the dope. We'll talk, we'll play a game or two. I just want to leave it all behind.»

goodbye the ship is sinking
rat

Douglas concealed his annoyance. This man was not not anyone, feelings had to be

dealt with

«I do understand. It's okay.»

to be that way when you need nothing
when you are so

«I can see more clearly now. I dont want the confusion. Being straight is a real high for me now. It's appreciated, Dougie. But just mistimed.»

his time mistime
not mine

«Listen, how about giving me a lift into town instead. There's something I've got to do.»

Douglas nodded, as he put the gift back in his pocket.

1215
THE BARGAIN'S STRUCK
castaway in sumptuous envy
**button-pushing
surmising on
the curious warmth
OF A BLOATED STOMACH
FORGET CONTRACTUAL DIFFICULTIES**

feed me
fold me over
lick and stick
me
down

I'll stay
in a specific locality
in your pocket
in love with what you have
to offer
to the wandering ray
inside me
thinking

here was this Kathy Pringle girl he'd met the other night at the Venue said she might be able to help him out with a room over in St Leonards

ok spot

She was an art student or a painter or something, a rich kid with a yen for the bohemian life. Ray provided her with an opportunity to indulge in it a bit. It looked like she had really gone for him. He didnt have to do a thing, she was the seducer, even bought the condoms at the all night garage and took him back to her place for the business. In the morning she was game for more but there was something about her, it was too easy, made him feel like he was being toyed with and he didnt like that. People getting ideas about you and how they could use you. But the flat was neat, plenty of room and handy for everything. It was worth thinking about. Though she wasnt his type, too wee and round, all hips, it was worth thinking about

> seriously folks but
> careful not to get trapped

Or maybe he should go and see the doo man. The old guy hadnt turned up this morning at the buroo. Maybe he was ill or something. There were two ways to go and Ray was not going to make any decision but just turn whatever corner his feet did because

> the head is not to be trusted
> as a guide for the whole
> any more than the heart

But the rain came on, drops like tiny comets with icy centres, stinging his face. Cursing the weather, he pulled his collar up around his neck and ran as fast as he could into the park, his duffle-bag bouncing up around his ears as he half walked half slid his way across the puddled grass. Decision made by circumstances.

By the time he reached the shelter of the buildings at St Leonards on the other side, his feet were freezing. His shoes were leaking badly. He stood for a while in the doorway of a bookies, out of breath, getting his bearings. The other night in the dark, he was drunk, she had led the way and he had been distracted by her dragging him up closes to squeeze his balls every hundred yards or so to pump up the action.

He was a bit annoyed at himself for not having got more out of her, about who she was, what she might be able to do in the way of useful connections. Ok it was obvious she had money, but the thing was, how serious had she been about helping him? Did she really fancy him, or was it all just a part of some game she was playing, being the bad girl who'd go back to mum and dad when they'd suffered enough?

> i really love you
> mother father
> and i'm sorry
> for what i've done
> when do I get the inheritance?

Still it might just be the chance to get out. Erchie was getting worse. He did nothing to keep the place clean, hardly washed or changed his clothes anymore. And all the old girl's stuff was still lying scattered about the place. Her room had never been touched at all. It wasnt as if he was in mourning or anything, he was down the boozer as soon as he had a quid in his pocket, buy one cadge two

>   sing them a song
>   a song of yore
>   Jolson Sinatra
>   if he needs one more

But this Kathy Pringle might be the very out he was looking for. The great thing was to maintain the cool. If he felt himself losing it, he'd tell himself to shut up or sit down, or say what was on his mind or something. If she was in. Maybe he should have tried phoning.

It took a while to find the street and the flat. For some reason he'd forgotten it was a basement flat, and he walked past it twice before he noticed the number. The flat had a light on in it and he chapped. After a moment, the door opened. It wasnt her but another woman, a bit older than Kathy and considerably more gorgeous, so much so it took his breath away for a second

>   there is more than one thing
>   to covet here

–Yes?

–Eh, I'm looking for Kathy Pringle, Ray said, straightening up and speaking as clearly as he could.

–I'm afraid she's out, came the reply. –I'm sorry.

Ray cursed under his breath. Typical. A line of water was trickling down from his head, under his collar and down his neck. He decided to give it a proper go

>   because
>   this is the chance
>   the door
>   that might open

–Listen, he said, –Kathy asked me to come round. Can I wait or something? It's pouring out here.

There was a pause, a sigh, she looked him over, then the vision spoke again.

–I suppose so. She said she would be back before lunch, so she shouldnt be long.

Inside, out of the rain, he shook the drops of ice from his hair. –You look soaked, she said.

–Aye, just a bit.

She led him into the hall, and went into a kitchen, telling him to follow. It was a big room with a fluorescent strip in the ceiling. The light from it was so bright, it hurt his eyes at first. Once he could focus, he noticed that the place was in a state of

A Day at the Office

disrepair. Some of the floorboards were up and wires stuck out from the holes. A lot of cardboard boxes with self assembly units in them were stacked against one wall. The woman was standing in front of a sink that was propped up by two small wooden crates, and looked as if it was hanging off its piping.

–She's having the kitchen done, she said, gesturing to the boxes. –New units. See if you can find a place to park yourself. I was just going to make some tea. You look as though you could do with a cup.

Ray stared at her. She was gorgeous
                            breathtaking
                              heart too
                    possibility out of reach?
                              o cupid
                       draw back your bow
                              and let
                        your arrow flow

–Aye, please, he said, –If it's no bother.

She picked up an electric kettle and turned around to fill it at the sink. He clocked the shape of her body through her clothes. Gorgeous. That arse, that hair. The curve of her neck. He couldnt take his eyes off her.

She went to plug the kettle in, noticed his expression and stopped.

–What are you looking at? she said, standing there with this challenging expression on her face. Embarrassed, he dropped his head, then looking up again, he frowned.

–Eh, I might be wrong but dont I know you from somewhere?

She shrugged and set the kettle to boil, leaned back against the sink and folded her arms. –I dont think so, she said. Her coolness intimidated him. He felt he had to explain something.

–No, maybe not, maybe I've just seen you somewhere.

He smiled –Maybe sat next to you on a bus or something, know what I mean? It's just a feeling.

The kettle began to hiss.

–Sometimes, she began, –Sometimes I get the feeling somebody's eyes are on me, it's like I can really feel it. On a bus or something, she said, then took two mugs down from where they were hung on pegs, alongside the sink

                    no wonder
                you're the wonder
                 worth looking at
   Ray blinked. He looked away. She gave a funny giggle and leaned back on the sink, which suddenly let out a loud creak as it tipped slightly under the pressure.
   –Whoops, she said, getting off it.
   –Doesnt look too secure, Ray suggested. She put two teabags in the mugs and disconnected the boiling kettle from the flex. He felt sure he knew her, but couldnt think from where. She was a good bit older than him, he reckoned. Maybe it was from school.
   –You're no from Eastercraigs, are you? he asked. She turned and shook her head.
   –No. Why, should I be?
   –It's just I'm sure I've seen you somewhere.
   For a moment she stared at him like she was weighing him up, whether or not he was ok. Then she poured the hot water into the mugs and turned towards him again.
   –Lennox, she said. –But I've not really lived there for years. It was like she was making a confession to him.
   –Lennox? Ray smiled. –So that's it. Did you go to the High School?
   She shook her head. –No. I went to St Thoms. Catholic. Sugar?
   Ray nodded his head, he knew where she meant.
   –How many?
   –What?
   –Sugars?
   –Oh no, no sugar. She gave an odd look as she fished out the teabags and put a drop of milk in both mugs, then she walked over and handed one to him.
   –So what are you then? A painter? she asked, sitting down on one of the boxes, sipping from her tea.
   –Me? He wasnt sure what she was on about.
   –There's nobody else here.
   Ray smiled. –Do you mean an artist painter or a painter and decorator painter?
   –Does it make a difference?
   –Sure. But the answer is no anyway.
   He took a drink from his cup. –You never told me your

name.
—Still trying to pin me down?
—Do you mind?
—I resent any encroachment on my free spirit, such as sounds that are supposed to reflect my personal identity, she said in a posh voice. For a moment he thought she was serious.
—But I'm, anyway, like it or not, Brenda McKenzie. What about you? Ray did you say? She was just winding him up.
—Aye. Ray Craig, he replied. Brenda McKenzie. It was familiar. —You got a brother called Paul?
She shook her head. —Still trying to place me?
Ray laughed. He pulled his tobacco out. Should he roll a j? If she lived with Kathy, it must be cool.
—I've got a wee bit of swag here if you fancy a blow. But her reaction was dead cold.
—Is that what you've to see Kathy about then? The way she said it, it sounded like dog shit. He was getting the picture, and decided to lie

> when in shtuck
> best policy
> for government

—No, I only met her the other day and she said I was to come round. I'm interested in em, painting.
She didnt seem convinced. She frowned.
—But you're not a painter?
—No, not really. But I do drawings.
Her face brightened, so he added a measure more.
—Weird drawings.
It was what she wanted to hear.
—Like.. em ... Bosch.
—Are you planning to exhibit, then?
—Exhibit?
—The gallery.
—Gallery?
—The Cooperative Gallery

> something not known about
> bluff it

—Oh aye.
—You're one of the group, are you?
Ray decided not to push it

> cant lie to someone
> so stunnin

> this is love not politics

—Well, no. I'm no, you know, professional. I just do a bit when I feel like it, know what I mean?

But she was still looking at him like he had to give some more away.

—I dont know. I dont have much finished work at the moment.

—You didnt bring anything with you?

—Not in this rain.

They drank their tea in silence for a minute or two. She looked at her watch.

—Typical Kathy. She's never back when she says she's going to be.

It was his cue to ask, —What time is it now?

—Twenty to, she yawned as she glanced at her watch.

—So what do you do then, Brenda? You a painter too?

—No. I've got no pretensions in that line.

The way she said the word pretensions seemed to give a lot away. Was that how she saw Kathy and her friends. If so, had he misinterpreted

> may be ok
> the way i phrased it
> casual
> like that

She drained her tea cup.

—I work in a bookshop.

—Yeah? What's that like then?

—I like it fine. I havent been there all that long, but it's quite interesting.

—I suppose you get a lot of time for reading.

—You're joking. It's not just books we sell, you know, it's everything. You never get a chance to stop and read the things. It might as well be shoes or something.

She was radiant. Brown eyes
> breakdancing
> body pop
> pop my way

—Yeah?

—Yeah. All you ever do is parcel them up and give the sales spiel.

> she was laughing
> and we are together

A Day at the Office

                    talking
                  not putting out
                       oh i
                      i ray
                could get to like this
   The sound of someone coming in made them both turn to
the door. It was Kathy. She came in clattering clumsily, not
seeing him at first.
                    is this her?
                did I really go her way?
   Maybe it was the contrast of the two women, one so calm
and lovely, advertising nothing of herself but sphinxing his
eye, the other huffing hardly able to contain that self within
her body, but Ray flushed red when he saw her and the
delighted look she gave him.
   –Ray!
   –Hiya Kathy, he answered without any enthusiasm.
   She came over to where he was sitting among the bits of
kitchen units and kissed him, boldly. Brenda was watching, he
could see her smile past the side of Kathy's head, and he felt
shamed to think of the other night and the ideas he had
entertained about some future relationship between them. It
wasnt that he had done anything wrong but he had been
tempted to, and if it hadnt been for Brenda he might have
done.
                 the choice was never so clear
                 between the attainable scorn
                  and the unreachable ideal
                  that maybe with patience
                       with virtue
                 if I went away and changed
                      to someone else
                someone good and honest maybe
   –Wow. She finally let him go.
   –You beast!
                  but no it's not that way
                        Brenda
                  it's not the way it looks
   –This guy had me falling asleep all day Friday at work, she
said to Brenda, staking her claim on him and Ray was yielding
                    what can I say but
                         sigh
                      it's beyond
                       it's gone

and he knew that it was time to go.

−I'd better be off, he said. He put the empty mug down and went towards the door. Kathy turned to him to mount a serious complaint, he should have been able to say something clever, he wanted to for Brenda, but there was nothing doing
just go
get out
while you can man
you'll look stupider staying

The rain had stopped outside and the wind had dropped away to a whisper. Ray went down the steps onto the pavement again. He walked quickly, not bothered by the squelching of his leaky shoes through the puddles. She was gorgeous, maybe not so untouchable, he had to
believe
that though

A bus would come, a twenty-one, and it would take him back to Eastercraigs for a while, but he was moving now. He could sense it.

A Day at the Office

1257

sneak away to queue
for take-out-eat-away
eatables
what matters it if i am seen
if dignity is tied to
conscience
if all is lost at all
the sustenance of bread is no
illusion
my jaws apart
i bite
i grind

the hunger stays me

ti
ecrof sgnieb elohw a seriuqer
to swallow

sometimes i feel about to
self combust
the overseer summarises
STAFF ALWAYS UNRELIABLE
STUCK IN A PERPETUAL RUT
REPEATING SHORT SCANT PHRASES
HARDLY MOVING
NO HOPE OF PROGRESS

but the morsel slides
acids attack
THE SYSTEM WORKS

my being becomes a chariot
a double decked moving tower
of mind and body
on the bus going north across the river, cutting a curve through the city centre to Lennox where her family had always lived, she had the sensation of time travelling
back

It was a journey she had made many times, home from school in blazer and skirt, crossing from a world in which she was the disadvantaged, where her uniform was cleaner but older than anyone else's, into a world where she was the privileged one, where the uniform was its mark
>					the colour
>					marooned
>					was she

In Lennox, the uniform made her stand out as different. At school it felt like it was the only thing she had in common with the other girls. There was a system of codes of behaviour, secret signals and key words that the others all seemed to know from years before
>					prepped
>					kept safe
>					a class
>					in kind

Maybe she should have asked more questions, maybe she should have just substituted their conventions for the ones she grew up with. But she had been intimidated by her ignorance, at primary school, at home, she had been the prizewinner, and she did know if she gave in to them her life would become a routine of insults. So she resisted being made to feel inferior, telling herself that if any of them had come out to Lennox, they'd have been chased back home in seconds
>					the YLT
>					ir efter ye

But they never did come. They had no need to. It was beneath them. Sure they may have been scared of its hard reputation, but to them that didnt count as something to be proud of. She was stuck in their world, and no longer a part of her own. She begged her mum and dad to let her leave but no, they just kept on saying what an opportunity it was, how few kids in the scheme got that chance
>					to be other
>					than mother
>					to the ache of repetition

Well it had ruined her for learning, that was for sure. Three weeks into the first term, she started the first fight in the memory of any teacher working there. The nuns were horrified
>					aflutter
>					with utter

>   disgust
>
> After that she was just bad. Not interested. Could do better. Yet the thing was she knew she could have done it, the whole academic trip, if she had wanted to, if the system hadnt spewed her back out
>
>   with nowhere to go
>
> Funny how it still irked, ten years on. She resented caring about it now, she wanted to leave it behind, but this bus trip was all it took to set the projector reeling back the memories.
>
> So she tried not to make the trip any more than she felt she had to. Today was the first in three months. It wasnt home, that word was just a habit
>
>   of mind or maybe heart
>   thou art weakening
>   reawakening
>
> The bus topped the hill and began to descend the gentle slope into the valley where Lennox lay. She thought again how beautiful it must have been before the planners moved in and carved the landscape up with their lines. Their blueprints and concrete mixers. She saw it in her imagination as a place naturally enchanted, where wild creatures would have come to drink the clear water of the burn.
>
>   a garden in this shallow indentation between hills
>   now cemented and overrun with people
>
> And it was still beautiful. If you lifted your eyes above the level of the street, if you looked at the curve of the hills. The air was cleaner here too, the exhaust fumes didnt choke you every few strides like they did up the town. The wind blew through the place without getting caught up in the buildings as happened with the tenements in Blacklands. But that wasnt the way most citizens saw it. The reality they were sold was one of no work, drinking, brawling, stealing, addicts and AIDS. But there was more, far more to this place than that. It was a whole microcosmic world, complete in itself to the kids who grew up there. Only when confronted with the wider perspective did they develop the critical attitude towards their home. And in embracing that critical view, they attacked themselves, their own sense of wellbeing, their own dignity. Maybe it had got worse since her time. She didnt know for sure. But it was the place where she had grown and she still felt warmth towards it
>
>   I cant not know it

>   let the cock crow it
>   thrice
>   unacknowledged

The bus stopped, walking the last hundred yards, the faces on the street were familiar. Some, recognisable, caused names long buried to re-emerge, but she didnt speak them, or say hello to those who bore them. It was a thing beyond word contact, this time travelling, and she was still somehow invisible, alone in the place that had wanted her to get out, to succeed, to show the world outside the world inside her, being Lennox and them. But this had placed her in no woman's land, it could not be understood by those who remained within the security of their own territory, and maybe like some eyes suggested she had given up her birthright, in adopting a place and a voice other than this native one, by submerging her childhood culture in a mass of other influences. Maybe she had sold out. But then she hadnt wanted to go in the first place. The leaving had been forced upon her. And it was her, not these faces, who had been exiled

>   from the cosy womb of insularity
>   our tradition

She came to Marischal Place, the houses as they had been, but less vivid than she remembered them, the paintwork shabby, the gardens untended. She thought of her father's struggle to turn the common back green into a source of vegetables, and his lengthy partnership with disappointment and vandalism. Yes she would keep these thoughts close, at heart they would always be, and she would visit now and then, but that is all

>   I dont know now
>   how to feel
>   since there is more than this
>   and more than this view
>   this outerinterference
>   between I and me
>   one and many
>   numbs

Steeling herself in this way, she climbs the stairs, the past alive in the present

>   tense
>   for why
>   pourquoi?

Six flats, central stairs, smell of cooking onions. She rings the

doorbell. Of course he will be in
>	faither
>	father
>	all in a vowel
>	that difference

'Helen!'
>	arms embrace
>	bodies link
>	squeeze
>	loose

'Dad.' The word a compromise, a name she never called him in her youth, but fitting now, that space of otherness.

'I thought it might be you, I was out on the balcony. But my glesses, ken, they're just for readin. Come in, come in.'

She enters a world where shapes and smells are still and all the same.

'Well, go in the kitchenette, your mother's watchin one of her soaps.'
>	meaning
>	she still has not
>	forgiven
>	leaving Colin

'Irene? Helen's here.' He shouts, the echo
'Helen's here?'
'So how're you gettin on, girl? It's a while since you were last down.'
>	slip
>	down

'Fine Dad, fine.'
>	why so empty?
>	words

'You're still in that flat at Blacklands?'
'Yes, still there. You'll need to come and visit.'
>	pointless invitation
>	token only

'Aye oh aye, we will, it's just your mother, ken, she's no that mobile now. No that she ever was, eh?'

He is putting the kettle on
>	new
>	the kettle
>	new the cups are too
>	nose like a bird's
>	hooked beak
>	not mine
>	my maw's is more

and whistling as he does it
　'So what's new, girl? Any news?'
　　　　　　　　　　　　these news
　　　　　　　　　　　but all's old
　'Not really. Just working, you know.'
　'That casino?'
　　　　　　　　　　　only nod
'Pssh … '
　　　　　　　　　but he shakes head
　　　　　　　　　sighs
　'Irene, do you want a cuppa?'
　　　　　　　australian soap washing cleaner whites
　　　　　　　　　no race relation
　'Your mother, ken, she's still not happy about you and Colin. I mean, Helen, you were doing so well, it's hard for her to understand why you'd want to walk out on him like that. That wee house you had in Linmill, it was rare. A dream for her, ken.'
　'He punched me, Dad, you know that.'
　'Sure sure, I know.'
　　　　　　　but does it mean the same to you
　'But couples have their disagreements, it's never perfect, girl.'
　'I didnt expect it to be perfect, only a bit better than it was.'
　'Pssh … '
　　　　　　　　　　　that noise
　　　　　　　　　　his noise
　　　　　　　　　exasperated
　　　　　to be followed by the shake of the head
　　　　　　　　　yes there it is
　'Irene, do you want a cuppæ tea?'
　　　　　　　　　echoes
　'Aye ok …
　'I mean what is it you're plannin tæ dæ, æ?'
　'Live the way I want tæ.'
　　　　　　　　　　　dæ
　'An what exactly is that, the way you want?'
　'I didnt come here to argue. I was hopin you'd have left off this by now.'
　　　　　　　　　but will you
　　　　　　　　　ever
'Pssh …'
　　　　　　　　　shake

A Day at the Office

The kettle's hiss blends with his, the switch clicks off, steam puffs camouflage
      he turns away
 'Irene, where did you put the teabags?'
            'They're in the tin.'
'No they're no.'
              'Aye they are.'
'Whit tin do you think they're in?'
           'The Millar's assortment.'
'The Millar's assortment. Since when did you keep the teabags in there?'
        'Oh shut up Tom, I'm tryin tæ listen.'
'Are you no comin in tæ see Helen.'
       no answer
       speak
'It's ok, Dad.'
       is it all that can be said
      not perfect but could do better
'I'll be through in a wee while. It's just comin tæ a good bit.'
'So you've not seen him then?'
'No. There's no point. I'm not wantin to go back.'
'I see.'
      but do you
'Well, I suppose she'll get used tæ the idea. She'll be ok, Helen. Just give her a bit of time. She'll forget about it.'
      but will you
and
      do I care
and
      if I dont care
does that mean I dont care for the bit of me that lingers here
    in your faces and expressions
'It's no as if we'd ever try to make your mind up for you, girl. But there's times, you ken, you see your kids, cos you still are to us, you ken, a kid, you see them doing things and realise that they dinnæ ken that you can make a move that seems so simple at the time, but when you look back on it, it's like it was the biggest kinda jump fæ one part o your life into another. I mean I look back now and think well maybe if we hadnæ done that then, then we'd be happier now.'
      more words together strung
     than I remember him as able to

       and he's makin sense
        tæ somethin in me
         but
'There's always that feeling in me, I cant say there's not. But..'
        is she listening
        in there listening
'I feel better now I'm out of it. I was just a kid then, dad, an maybe you still look at me an see me like that still, but I've grown up a lot. I know for you an mum that what I had with Colin seemed a good thing, but it was his, all his, you see, no bit of it was really mine.'
 'You cannæ look at marriage that way. It's a partnership, girl.'
 'Ideally maybe. It wasnt that way for us.'
        will she not come in
        is she ignoring me
 'Psshaw ... '
He looks up to the door, where Helen's mother has appeared.
        oh maw
 'Helen. How're you?'
        cold cold cold
 'Ok. How're you?'
 'Och næ bad. Bothered wi arthritis, but that's nothing new now is it?'
 'No. But still you're keeping no too bad?'
 'Aye ... '
      cold spaces between words
      incalculably frozen time gaps
       suspending us untouching
 'Are you staying for yer dinner?'
 'No I've got to get back.'
She nods her head, as if
        she knew
 'Is that tea no ready Tom? You'll have time for a cuppa though?'
 'A quick one.'
       though it will be so slow
       and it will be cold even if
        it steams and burns
        it will not warm me
 'Get the biscuit tin down, Tom, I cannæ reach it.'

A Day at the Office

He turns and pulls the tin down from the shelf above his head.
>they keep everything in tins
>and keep every tin
>to keep things in
>they are the keepers
>of my sense of sin
>and I cant bear to be in their sin tin
>reduced to kid talk thought
>like this
>the always less than really hereness
>of it

'Have you seen Stuart lately?'
>the lead up

'No not for a while.'
'But you're still there in that bedsit place he got you?'
'Still there aye.'
The biscuits are opened and placed on centre table, digestives, rich tea and the chocolate ones
>that are the test
>of just how much I'll take from them
>to take
>one chocolate one's polite
>two means I need something
>and three means feed me save me

Helen took one digestive from the tin. Her mother sat down at the table facing her. The tension was visible on her
>she might have blamed on the pain
>on her arthritis

but she couldnt hide it.
'Is that the place belongin tæ the brother of the lad Stuart used tæ ken, him that killed himsel?'
>nod
>understood with nod

'I pity his poor mother, ken? Whit a thing tæ hæ tæ live wi, æ?'
'It's been a while now. A couple of years. Douglas seems to be getting over it.'
>first name terms betray

'Douglas? That's the brother is it?'
'His younger brother.'
'An he's the one you're rentin this flat fræ?'
'Yes.'
>not aye

'I see.'
The tea and biscuit ritual is broken by the tv news. Her father leaves the room to listen, leaving
us
alone
Her mother dips a rich tea in her cup.
'So you're alright are you, Helen?' peeking at her side-e-ways.
'I'm doing ok. I was saying to dad, I'm doing fine.'
'And Colin, do you see him?'
'No not for a while.'
Maw
cannot approve of me
not being maw
Helen knew that she could only go away now. The space that had been hers in the time when she and Colin had been courting, when they had been given the couch on which to make their bond, right here in this flat, that was all gone now. She had no choice but to leave. She had never had any choice but to leave, and in going forwards lay the only hope of future happiness. She had to make a chariot of her life and set it rolling through the years, and maybe, maybe in the future once this time had faded into herstory, they would forgive her for rolling over all the rutted tracks in which their own old wheels had stuck.

1331
the shuffling train
beneath this park
tunnels deeper
than i want to go

the thought that i could lose
this place as lightly
as i came to live it
leaves me dashing for my desk
my place of doubt
my work

MY OFFICE

*securing fingerless deposits
in your numbered credit
hoarding spot*

the secret place of business
where the dealer dodges justice through a thin fog drifting up the river from the sea, oozing out of fissures in the grey dome of cloud hanging over the city, as Douglas drove down the Great Western Road through the suburbs, into the centre of the
black heart land
As he neared Tollcross, the busy, narrow streets were suddenly lit up by a bright New Year sales shopping display. He turned right at the cross, and headed over towards Blacklands. In the back of the car, he had stacked a number of boxes containing his purchases from his London trip. A few pieces he would sell through his contacts in the antique trade. But the real purpose for his trip, the package of coke that would set his west end friends abuzz was safe in his mother's house. He parked in front of his shop and waited for a moment before getting out. This was the nerve wracking part of the deal, these few hours between getting the stuff and delivering it to the outlets. He felt the familiar surge of adrenalin
the tumbling stomach
He got out of the car and went to the hatchback door,

opened it, picked up the box and set another on top. He turned and began to descend the steps to the basement entrance, and as he was doing so, he caught sight of two men getting out of a parked car further down the street and coming towards him. He looked away quickly, momentarily lost his nerve, then stumbled on the steps
> wet sole

They were still coming in his direction, headed straight for him. But they seemed too casual in their approach to be drug squad. He calmed himself and put the key in the shop door lock
> deliberate

«Mr Shaw?»

Feigning surprise, he turned to face them.

«Yes?»

They came down the steps. He sighed heavily as the first one produced his ID. The box that had contained the coke was on the ground at his toe, but it was
> superbly
> completely
> wonderfully empty.

«Would you mind answering a few questions, sir?»

He repressed the natural urge to become defensive.

«Questions?»

His head was speeding
> burning
> it was a surge of current
> like ECT

but he managed to smile and say quite idly, «What about?»

The spokesman of the two came down to where Douglas stood. He was quite a small man.

«You obviously havent heard, then, about the incident?»

«No, what incident?»

«A woman in the block next door to you was seriously assaulted – some time between nine o'clock last night and seven this morning.»

Douglas tried hard to appear concerned, and not to show his relief though
> to know it's not me weaks

«Really? It's the first I've heard of it. Is she all right?»

«Too early to say yet, sir. We're just making inquiries at the moment. To find out if anyone saw anything.»

A Day at the Office

«Well I'm afraid I cant help you there. I've only just got back from a business trip to London. But if you'll give me a minute, I'll just put these boxes in the safe, and then if I can assist in any way, I am at your disposal.»

The policeman seemed annoyed by his tone.

«Valuables, sir?»

cut the nose
to spite the face

Douglas lifted the boxes from the ground and gestured towards the sign over the door.

«Antiques,» he said as he crossed the threshold.

To his annoyance, they made to follow him inside, but he didnt show his displeasure, he simply took the boxes to the office and safely locked them out of sight. Through the crack between the door and its jamb, he watched them snooping about. As he came out into the front shop again, the second policeman spoke.

«Not much of a stock at the moment, sir? I'd half hoped to pick something up while I was here. I'm a keen amateur collector. Anything a little unusual, curios.»

killed the cat

He stared hard at Douglas, who couldnt suppress a laugh.

«I'm just about to begin refitting the shop,» he answered. «But I dont keep much stock on the premises anyway. I'm not that involved in the retail end of the trade.»

The first of the two resumed the lead.

«We understand you own the flats above as well, sir?» he said, peering into the office through the open door.

«That's correct,» Douglas answered. He was imitating their own formal intonation

one of you but not sirring

«All rented out, are they?»

«All but my own.»

«And which is that, sir?»

«The ground floor – directly above.»

«A legacy, wasnt it? Thats what we heard, wasnt it?» He turned to his sidekick for confirmation, then stared at Douglas as if he was thinking, rich brat.

«That's right.» Douglas said no more, but waited.

«One of your tenants, a Mr Richard Harris. Know where he might be?»

So that was it. Ricky. They must have figured him as a likely suspect but he was
miles away
clean
Douglas shook his head, whistled thoughtfully.

«Sorry, I cant say for certain but I believe he's on holiday abroad at the moment. I don't really have much to do with the tenants,» he said. «All that's taken care of by an agency. I'll give you their card.»

He took out his wallet and fished out the agency card, from which all the leases originated
truly
«As far as Mr Harris goes, I've only really passed him in the stairway. He seems polite enough. You dont think he's involved in this business, do you?»

The first policeman shrugged. «We have to check everything out, sir. I'm sure you understand.»
too well
«Yes of course. Well, call on me at any time, if I can give you any help.»

«When Mr Harris turns up, could you get him to give us a call at the station?»

When they left, with thanks on their lips for his help, he knew that underneath they were irked by their failure to intimidate him. He began to laugh as the adrenalin that had seeped through his body tingled
soothed
releasing natural opiates
athletes crave
He heard a car start up and pull away, unworried. Did policemen really have a sixth sense for crime? Had they sniffed him out? It was all a bit too close for comfort, but it was beautifully thrilling.

Looking at his wristwatch, he realised he had opened the shop on time for once, unwittingly. But it was raining hard outside, and the street would be empty. He went to the door and picked up the mail from the mat. Some of the letters were a bit damp. The driving wind had caused a small flow of water to slip under the door. He went to his desk and mopped the wettest with a tissue. Then his eye fixed on the one beneath it in the pile, and he picked it up along with the letter opener. He

A Day at the Office

recognised the official stamp, and slit the top with a sense of already having seen
the money man
It was another request for him to visit his bank manager, drawing attention to the fact that Mr Shaw had failed to deposit any funds despite repeated promises and that he was now in debt to this branch by over seven thousand pounds. This state of affairs was quite unacceptable and would he please contact him to arrange an appointment as soon as possible
discard discord
Douglas didnt finish reading the letter. It was just the usual mixture of banker's threat and formal politeness. But something would have to be done. Justice would have to be seen to be done. Worst of all was the thought that his mother would get to hear about it. It was her bank too, and she was on friendly terms with the manager. It was quite conceivable that he would get in touch with her. And if he did, she would be round at the shop the next day
issuing ultimatums
asking questions about the money he had borrowed from her under the pretence of using it to set his gallery on the road to success. She would want to know where that cash had gone. He couldnt tell her the truth, that it was wrapped up in the biggest coke deal he had ever tried to pull off, that at this very moment the missing tenant was hopefully finalising the arrangements. He could only trust
gambler's instinct
let it ride for another turn of the wheel
Ricky was days late, but not so late as to be a real cause for concern. And if and when it all came through, the money would be quadrupled at least, even with expenses. But this was the way
if you want to win big
you have to take the risks
His own grandfather had been a compulsive gambler but had built the foundation of the family wealth, not to mention half the district. Today things were different only in terms of the commodity, the same principles applied. Douglas saw himself like his grandfather in many ways, both the second son who had inherited when the elder brother died. His

grandfather knew how to buy and sell at a profit.

It was the lack of security that bothered him, and the fact of lying to his mother. But the odds were unbelievable. The thing was to remain calm at all costs. There was no point losing his nerve now. In a few weeks, this whole dreadful time would be nothing but a memory. He could bluff it a bit longer. What was in his reach was worth more than any other single thing he had ever held before, and it wasnt going to be small time any longer, he would
cut myself into the big league
The package at mother's is only the beginning
Ok it's not easy to

pull it off. His somersaulting stomach had tilted his mind when the deal was done, and the drive north had been freaky at times, monitoring his speedo and watching for every potential blue light hiding place. It was only powder, he kept telling himself
a herbal extract

it had no power without a mind to work on. It was only
time to have a line
mirror
blade
the gentle chopping
sweeping edge across smooth glass
every dot visible
scrape it
scrape it
make it right
length
breadth
the toot tube

He took half of it into his left nostril, then a breath, a smile, then the other half into his right
just right
beautiful
tingling
numbing rush
seconds ticking
the moment
now
music
magic flute toot
more Mozart for good measure
music
wonderful soothing

                        smoothing
            what it could do was joyous
                        soulful
                        inspiring
                no need for words.
                Simply relax indulge
                these moments fully
            tangential bombardment of ideas
                too fast to hold on to
            All these marvellous what ifs?
            Take a pencil and draw a symphony!
                    Ha! Sonata form
                        But Helen
            Oh she would be coming in soon
                ghosting through the door
                        my door
                pleasure unbounded
                delicious flesh grass
                    young and sapful
                        that girl
                    picking her luck
            there is something going on here
            beginnings of an end means towards it
                        Siddhartha
        that copy in Dutch with the psychedelic cover
                een indiese vertelling
                where was it now but

It was the phone
                        that buzzing.
«Hello. Shaw Antiques?»
«Dougie?»
«Yes?»
                    that faraway voice
                through a subterranean hollow.
«It's Rick. I'm in Amsterdam.»
«Wow. That's really you? That's incredible. I was just thinking about ... »
                    Oh never mind
                    synchronicity again
                    Dutch Amsterdam.
«What?»
«Forget it. What's happening?»
«Everything. Smooth as planned. Nothing agley.»
«What about the silver?»
«It's on its way. I paid a wee bit more than we reckoned, but it was easy, man. What a thrill. I could really get to like this

business.»

«Whohoah! You mean it?»

«Easy like I say. Listen, I'll see you shortly. I'm going to take the long way round. Fingers crossed for the final lap.»
     composure
     coolness

«Sure. Take your time. You deserve a holiday. Let me know by letter when and where. Ok?»

«Ok. Listen, I've got to go. I'm meeting this wee Dutchie.»

«Of course. Thanks for calling.»
    so this was it then
     the moment
     Ricky delivers
   stupendously immaculately
    incomprehensibly right
      take a bow
      clap hands
     here comes Charlie.

1401
back
belly leaning on the edge
of this cosy three foot
precipice
i feel so manifestly safe
IF YOU'LL JUST SIGN HERE
I CAN EXTEND YOUR CONTRACT
THE PENSION SCHEME
CAN PROMISE YOU
SOME TRULY RICH REWARDS
FOR LOYALTY YOU'LL GLEAN
ANOTHER SPROUTING SPRING
FRESH APPETITE GREAT VIGOUR
THE POWER OF SELF-ASSERTION
NO HUMBLE TRADESMAN
MOCKS OUR STAFF
RIGHT NOW DISPOSE OF ALL
YOUR OLD ADDICTIONS
YOUR FEELINGS OF WORTHLESSNESS
THOSE WORN OUT WORRY BEADS
THE OPPRESSIVE RELIGION
THE LACK OF FAITH
BELIEVE IN THE COMPANY
but please dont fret
if you really want to keep
those useless crutches
we can arrange you start
a rehabilitation scheme
the end of which is guaranteed
to make your old bad habits
just as sweet and fresh
as when you first
so innocently found them
DO YOURSELF A FAVOUR
COME TO THE PARTY
dont live the hermit life
that solitary suffering
of i ray with his pain
that toothache

has been working on him for three days. It was a
hellwholehole
A cavity as big as a bean, he could fit the tip of his tongue in it. It should have been out long ago, but still the tooth was strong and he bit on it, chewed with it. It was a favoured instrument of mastication.

It's not that I'm scared
it's to do with
lying back
on the chair
mouth open
throat exposed
submitting
like a dug

But three days ago he made himself a sandwich, just bread and tuna from the fridge, and when he bit into it, the cold flesh of the fish touched the nerve

hjoingwol,rtvesxunrbytec864309oi 65rtim]
=-[hvm#
agony pure fucking
AGONY
kujotv;akp;oimy sp.dr¶p.or[.i,uyp¶oi/m
#[p0yh 4
like that
words are not enough

A bit stayed in there and he poked about in it with split matches and even went out to buy toothpicks, and he brushed and brushed, but despite dislodging bits the thing hurt more and more and painkillers by the bottle only made it feel like it was the only feeling in his body

only the pain

He knew all about that, from watching his mother's slow decline. Living on her nerves. If it had been him, he'd have found a quicker way, a bottle of pills or a swan dive down into the filthy river. But soon it would ease. Over and over the wilful optimism tried to smooth

pain brings death closer than sleep
in sleep we wish for fulfilment
in pain we seek only annulment
Yes i watched her die
daily biting cold to the nerve
suffering
martyred
a good christian soul

But something would have to be done. He couldnt just spend the rest of his life waiting for the toothache to subside. It reminded him of the time when he had stayed in his room waiting for his mother to die, only coming out to sign on, to eat, to score, to buy a thing or two, a book or record. Eighty-four. The doctors gave her six months. They were all waiting, Erchie, Ray, her

> in a stupor of bad taste
> of poison
> it's always slow poison
> life the dying process
> travelling over the city
> creating out of self
> an empty ruin

The number forty-five pulled slowly up the brae onto the shoulder of Torry Hill, from where a slope of scree and broom rose steeply to a crown of precipitous crags. It was a landmark Ray was well familiar with, but not at such close range, and he glowered at it in some awe. He was far from his usual haunts here, on a quest after blow. The chase had been complicated by just about the worst shortage he'd ever known. Everybody was dry, not just any wee clique, but everybody. A couple of big international busts were being blamed. He'd been chapping doors all over the place with no luck. Now it was down to a guy Gordie had told him about. He said he was a weirdo, hardly ever left his flat.

Glancing out the other side of the top deck, he saw the avenues of red sandstone tenements stretching out along the contours of the hill, stepped one above the other, like the rows of spectators at a football match. The view over the city, with the castle on its rock and the river below was beautiful. Watching the street names as they passed his eye, he found his target and got off at the first stop. He turned and walked back down the hill, till he came to the street he was after.

Along the road a bit, a gang of scaffolders were setting up the front of a block for sandblasting. A few of the other blocks had already been given the treatment, so that the street was kind of chequered. And further down again, a second gang were at work. The noise rang like thundering applause as he approached. Another part of the city lined up for renewal. More desirable spots to pitch a mortgage

mort
death
you take it to the grave
better off with a tent in the park
a cardboard box

It was maybe the nearest he'd ever get to a place uptown.

He found the close he was looking for. Top floor, Gordon had said. So he went up. And up. And up, and up. Eighty-eight effing steps, he was knackered. Left flat. The name was right. Togher. But the outside door was shut.

He rang the bell anyway, not keen to turn away without even trying it, after climbing all the way up there. Nothing happened, so he knocked in case the bell wasnt working. Loudly.

nothing doing
damn

He turned to go. But just as he was stepping down the first flight, he heard the lock being opened and the outside door cracked.

–Who is it?

Ray leapt up the steps again. –I was looking for Brian Togher.

An unshaven chin moved in the light from the roof window.

–He knows you, does he, this Togher?

Ray shrugged, –No, no really, but a mate said he might be able to help me out.

–Oh aye? Who is he then, this mate of yours?

–Big Gordon McQueen.

The door cracked open further. –And who are you?

–Ray. Ray Craig.

–Alright, Ray. I'll see if Brian's up.

The man beckoned him inside, and pointed to the kitchen, telling him to wait in there. The room was small and dark and in a helluva state. As he crossed over to the window, he tripped over a piece of torn lino. The floor was coming through it all over the place

more holes than lino

The sink was full of unscraped dishes and the table was covered in the tin foil container remains of a take-away, Chinese, judging by the half eaten bag of prawn crackers

what a pigsty
it was worse than Erchie's mess on giroday

A Day at the Office

Voices talking in loud whispers sounded from the hall.
–Fucksake man, you shouldnt have answered it.
–Och it's just some kid says he knows Gordon.

Togher came into the kitchen in his bare feet, buttoning the cuffs of a shirt which was ripped at one oxter, a wee man with a sour face.
–You looking for me, son? he said gruffly, as he switched on an uncovered light bulb. Ray was dazzled for a second.
–Aye. Gordon McQueen said you might be able to help me out. I'm after some draw.

Togher pulled out a chair and sat down at the table, sideways on to it. He cleared the debris with a sweep of his hand, then sighed.
–Stick on that kettle at your elbow, will you son? I've still no had a brew this morning. You're a helluvan early riser.

Ray located the kettle. It was near empty so he took it to the sink and tried to fit its spout between the tap and the pile of dirty dishes, which suddenly collapsed into the greasy water with a clatter.
–Mind that crockery, Togher grunted.

Ray glanced at him over his shoulder.
–No damage, he said, though he felt like dumping the lot on the floor, and he filled the kettle. Togher was rolling a joint at the table, holding a petrol lighter to a lump of hash, and when he had finished, he threw the lighter over to Ray. Ray put the kettle on the cooker and lit the gas.
–So you're a mate of Gordon's, right?
–Aye well I've known him a while. I went to school with him.

He lifted up the completed joint and gave Ray a look that said *I'm the one with the dope*. He lit the joint and took a long drag, then broke into a retching cough.
–First o the day, he spluttered, and he settled back to smoke. Ray was dying for him to pass it. The smell wafted over to him, overcoming the stink of cold chow mein and turning the dirty room into a nice place to be. But Togher didnt. He hogged it, savouring it, watching Ray's eager face get more desperate
the bastard
The kettle began to spout steam and Ray turned the gas off. Togher leaned over the table to an old radio cassette almost

hidden by the mess and switched it on. A sharp unmusical hiss blew out of the speaker, then faded.

—Fuckin thing's never worked, he grunted. —Bought it off my brother. Should have known better. He stood up, and finally passed the smoke to Ray. It was almost down to the roach.

—Make the tea, eh? It's up there in the press somewhere. I'm just away down to the corner for some milk and a breath of air.

Ray took another quick draw on the j and offered what was left back to him. Togher sniffed. —Just finish it, my lungs are killing me the day.

Alone in the room, he took his time over the last few puffs. It was good. Good to get it inside him, worth putting up with Togher for. Gordon had said he was a gangster, but he seemed more like a slob to Ray

<pre>   like a dozen other small time dealers i ray know
           who loved to make the customer grovel and beg
             folk who were so stuck in their situation
           theyd given up hope of ever getting into another
              old hippies who had cut their hair off
                but still lived in the prepunk era</pre>

He knew he was just a kid on the dole to Togher. That was fair enough. All that mattered was to get the blow and go.

The tea was made and the j long stubbed when Togher came back. There was somebody with him, a younger bloke with a neat grey suit, carrying a briefcase. Looked like he might be a lawyer or something. Togher was all smiles though. He came right into the kitchen and stuck a pint of milk into Ray's hand, then went over to the sink and pulled out three mugs from the water and ran them quickly under the tap. The bloke in the suit hovered on the threshold of the room.

—Want a brew, Douglas? Togher said. The man didnt reply but stayed in the shadow of the door, like he was afraid of catching something if he went into the room. Togher turned to look at him.

—Come on in, Douglas. I'm just making a cuppa.

Ray saw the beckoning nod as the man stepped back out of sight, in the dark of the hallway. Togher went out to speak to him. Their voices were low but Ray could hear them clearly enough. He reckoned probably he was meant to.

—What's up, Douglas?

–Two things, Brian. First, what's he doing here? Second, I thought I'd told you never to use my name in front of anybody.
There was a pause, then Togher laughed.
–Och come on, he's cool, man. I'll vouch for him.
But the man in the suit wasnt having it.
–I'm not interested in you vouching for him, I'm just telling you, this is your last chance. I dont like the way you do things. You're too slack.
–Slack? What do you mean, I'm slack? Eh? Togher's tone was angry.
–You're not discreet. I've said it before, Brian. This is it. Your last chance.
Then, with a decrying laugh, Togher turned on him.
–You think I need you? You think I really need you coming poncing in here? You think you're the only contact I've got?
Ray had had enough. He walked out of the kitchen, into the dark of the hallway. Both figures turned to look at him.
–Where are you going son? Togher growled.
Ray sighed. –I'm off. This is more than a smoke is worth, know what I mean? And he's right, you know. You are slack. He didnt mean to say it, but once it was out, he added. –And you're a slob too.
Ray stepped towards the door. Togher was mad now. He leapt forward and pinned Ray up against the back of the door in a half-nelson, so that his face was squashed into the coats hanging there.
–You're a cheeky wee cunt, are you no? he grunted, and tried to swing Ray round to face him, but Ray got an arm free and pushed him off. They stared at each other for a second, both ready to let loose, but the man in the suit stepped in between them.
–That's enough, Brian, he said seriously, but his voice wasnt firm like it should have been. Ray could see he was panicking.
Togher stood, breathing heavily, staring first at the man between them, then at Ray. His eyes were jumping about in his head.
–You fuckin stay out of this, Douglas. This is between me and the boy. Or I swear I'll do you too, dope or no dope.
–It's alright, Ray said. –I'm no feared for him.

The bloke in the suit looked nervously at them both, then meekly stepped out of the way. Ray felt the adrenalin pumping through his body. It was dark but he saw the move coming long before Togher made it, dodged his lunge and dumped him on the floor. He heard footsteps coming from another room and knew that Togher's friend would be there in a second. He let one sharp kick go, right into Togher's balls, and got out the front door as quick as he could. Ray clattered down the stairs, two at a time

> kids playing games
> gangsters my arse
> kids games just
> the smoke's not worth it
> no with that kind of shit about

Gordie had warned him alright. So he couldnt complain.

> but gangsters
> my arse

He heard the sound of someone coming down after him as he emerged from the close, so he ran quickly across the road to where the scaffolders were working and stood behind a skip where no one could see him. After a minute or so, the man in the suit came out and got into a smart silver hatchback parked outside. Ray waited a moment more, then started off walking down the street towards the bus stop

> so
> no dope then
> that was that
> Togher's off the list for good
> and one to watch out for

As he turned the corner onto the hill, a car came up behind him and started crawling the kerb. He glanced round, ready to take off. It was that silver hatchback. He decided to ignore it, and carried on walking, but the car pulled up beside him so he stopped. The driver leaned over and wound down the passenger side window. –Want a lift?

–I'm no hitching, Ray answered. He was still fizzing inside. The bloke in the suit opened the door. Ray looked up the street and down, then scratched his head. The bloke was leaning over, looking up at him

> a kind of silly smile on his face

He seemed totally harmless.

–So what's all this about then? Ray asked. –You didnt even want me to see you back there?

A Day at the Office

–That was before I was impressed by your mettle.
–My metal?
metal
iron
problems out
–You know, your prowess.
–You mean dumping that old duffer? Ray snorted. –Huh!
The driver shook his head. –No, seriously, I was impressed. Brian's had that coming to him for a while. You did me a favour. So how about that lift?
Ray sniffed. He was cooling out.
what about it?
nothing to lose
go for it
He got in the open door and pulled it shut.
–Seat belt, the bloke said.
–Oh aye sorry. He fixed it in place.
After a moment, Ray smiled –I was expecting the cavalry down the road after me, he said.
–I dont think Brian will be running anywhere for a while.
–What about his mate?
–He's probably rolling the first decent spliff he's had in a month right now. It's a strange thing, ganja. You'd sell your best friend for a good deal, wouldnt you? Or would you? They would, that's for sure. He looked at Ray with the same silly smile on his face.
But this time Ray noticed that there was a kind of wisdom there, like he had seen all this before, like he was a lot older than he looked, which was only about twenty-five.
–The guy's a mess, Ray said.
–Which guy?
–That Togher.
–Agreed. The car pulled out and he went quickly up through the gears, then let it coast down the slope. Ray frowned. He was curious.
–So what were you doing there?
–The same as you, I'd guess, but from the other end. Supplying, not buying.
He wasnt surprised, but it was weird to think that this suit and tie man was a big dealer. Though he had seen the movies, right enough, and was quietly happy to think he had made a connection.

but still it was weird

He checked. —You supply him?

—I did. But I think that Brian Togher has outlived his usefulness. He isnt discreet, he hesitated. —I dont know your name, do I?

—Ray, Ray answered. —Ray Craig.

The man lifted his right hand from the steering wheel and offered it over. —I'm Douglas, as you've already discovered, he said, shaking Ray's hand, —Douglas Shaw.

Ray decided to brass it. —So have you got anything then? Cause I've been all over, and there's nothing. The whole place is dry.

—Was dry, Ray. He pulled out a huge lump of hash neatly wrapped in cellophane from a pocket, it was more dope than Ray had ever seen in one piece, then stuck it out of sight again.

—You see, I'm the man to help you, Shaw said, and made this funny clucking laugh. Ray tried not to show his excitement.

—You usually carry stuff about with you like that?

—Oh no. Shaw shook his head. —This is delivery day. I dont like it, but it has to be done. And it isnt a task to be entrusted to just anyone. He gave Ray a very heavy stare. He understood what it meant, and met it with a slow nod

gotcha

Shaw smiled.

—Where are you heading for, Ray? he asked.

—Me? Och nowhere really. Then he laughed. —What I was looking for is right here.

Shaw clucked again. —Well where are you coming from then? he asked.

—Och nowhere, I've no roots, me. Just kind of float about. I've been looking for a place for a while now, but with the Housing Benefit cuts, it's not easy. I had a room in a flat over at Tollcross for a while.

—Are you unemployed then?

—You could say that.

The car reached the riverside and came to a stop at a set of lights. Ray looked out the passenger window. The water was murky, and racing downstream in a terrific rush after all the rain. Up above, the castle rock loomed over them, throwing a dark shadow like a cloud across the sun. Shaw pulled a small card out of his wallet and handed it to him. He read it. DOUGLAS SHAW: DEALER IN ANTIQUES AND OBJETS D' ART, it said, with an address in Blacklands and a phone number.

–That's an old one, Shaw said. –I havent got the new batch back from the printers yet, I'm opening a gallery soon. But the telephone number and the address is the same.

The lights changed, the car lurched forward.

–Very nice, Ray said and went to give it back to him.

–No no, I meant for you to keep it. Come round some time. If ever you think I can help you out. I feel I owe you a favour.

Ray sniffed. –Thanks. I will.

He pulled the string open on his duffle-bag and pushed the card inside the paperback he was carrying. Crossing the river, he looked down at the water again, running through in a rippling, interwoven pattern, under the bridge and out into the wide basin on the other side.

He felt happy just to sit there, going along with this Shaw guy, a weird sort of calm, as if he could just give up the choosing of direction and let this bloke take him with him

     on and on
    wherever he is going
  like I am adrift in the river current
     not swimming
     not struggling
     but floating

The car heater was blasting out warm air. The radio was on, playing some fancy classical music,

 the kind of thing the three musketeers would strut their stuff to
     bowing and bending
  elegant swinging of arms and feathered hats

–Can I drop you somewhere? Shaws voice broke into his dwam. They were on the north side of the river, opposite the castle, heading west. Ray sighed and waited

    where was the deal to be done?
   he could hardly cut and weigh a sixteenth
   sitting in a car in the middle of the High Street
   and I cant afford any more than a sixteenth

–Ray?

–Oh em sorry. Aye, anywhere here will do.

Shaw picked the first available spot and pulled in. Ray didnt want to get out, but it was obvious he had to. He looked around for the door handle.

—Eh, about the blow. he started. Shaw smiled, held out his closed fist, down low under the cover of the dash board.
—Hold your hand out, you naughty boy.
Ray stuck out his opened palm and in it Shaw dropped a lump, already wrapped, about the size of an eighth. Ray tried to hand it back.
—Look man, I cant afford this. I've only got enough for a sixteenth.
Shaw smiled. —Take it. Call it a gift.
Ray looked at it. He could taste it already. He shook his head in amazement, then got out of the car. Before he closed the door, he poked his head back inside.
—Thanks man. I dont know what to say. I mean ...
Shaw interrupted. —Say nothing. It's quite alright. Call round sometime. I might be able to help you again.
He put the car into first, looking impatient, like he was late for some appointment. Ray said —Thanks again, and shut the door. The car pulled out, to join the westward stream of traffic. Ray watched it go, expecting it to shoot off into the distance, but instead it pulled in again a hundred yards up the street.
Shaw got out of the drivers door and called out to Ray.
<blockquote>run or walk to him
how much to give back</blockquote>
Ray half jogged along the pavement.
—Ray, I've had a great idea. Jump in
<blockquote>the river and drown
great notions
Irene
goodnight</blockquote>
—What is it?
Shaw smirked. —A magical mystery tour, my friend
<blockquote>what to do now
the rippling tongue
of the river is calling
to take this chance
come out of this shell
be known to another
or stay on my own ground alone?</blockquote>
Ray got in.

1446
THE PRICE IS FIXED ACCORDING TO DEMAND
LET EACH ACCORDING THEIR MEANS DELIVER

i feel no pain
no sense of loss
despite this longing to be free
of certainty
wave   fist

s
u
r
r
e
n
d
e
r

self

to the wheel of fortune
like Helen think

it was inevitable
there's something to be had from that alone
the simple fact that things will happen
you've only got to move confidently
without doubt
guided by belief in the inevitability of things happening
like I did the day I walked out on Colin
it had nothing to do with coincidence
it was about concurrence.
things coming together,
not happening together
it's about trusting in fate
whether you believe in it or not
nothing's hard
worry
and the need to have something to worry over
that's the death of freedom
make no predictions but be aware of the moment and its potentials
let your feet take you there
dancing

avoid the unmentionables
like love
it's not a thing to think about
it's too hard to define
you can only define it by believing in it
but the need to support that belief
overcomes the feeling that gives birth to it
in time everything else crumbles
is made of sand
but to have this feeling
love or whatever
to want to nurture it
by not pressurising is the beginning of the end
you are inside it
that's the problem
you cant take your own good advice
or step outside love
moments spent in trying to avoid the known pitfalls
begin the process of pressurising dont they
is it a magical
neverending
going nowhere staircase
or what
when you think you're getting there
is it just an illusion
nowhere but older
and yet the going nowhere feelings
sometimes the most wonderful feeling
there is
if you could just take it and bottle it
like perfume
to wear like make-up
to have it always at hand
bottled
a secret
personal magic like that
bottled
sure thing is you cant
it isnt like that
you can only go
not to it like a place
but through it
more like a direction
in the going
there's the hope of finding
in the feeling of inevitability
there's a reason to keep going
and in the finding the surprise that you had always been going through it

A Day at the Office

> that you dont stop when you find it
> and things dont happen anyway
> they just come together
> like me and Douglas
> now

Helen turned away from the window. His flat was beautiful. He had so many beautiful things. She loved to just be in it, on her own like this, free to nose around

> these things
> do satisfy

He didnt appreciate how lucky he was, born into money, into the possession of things. But he did look after them. He was more houseproud than she was by far. Hoovering and polishing. It made her feel guilty. But she had had enough of that

> enough is enough is enough
> of that
> as good as a feast

The doorbell made her jump. She went through the hall and looked through the peephole. It was a woman she hadnt seen before, wearing a fur coat, with red rimmed yuppie glasses. She opened the door

> slowly
> counting one to ten
> time to become
> the person in residence

'Yes?'

The woman seemed surprised to see her there. 'Oh,' she said, 'I'm looking for Douglas Shaw. Does he live here?'

'Yes.'

> double yes
> makes a no
> who are you look

'I see.' A smile spread over her face

> calculated to engender
> good humour
> or
> baring the teeth

'And is he in at the moment.'

'No. He's out on business.'

> business is business

Helen weighed the caller up. American tinge to her tongue. She was younger than she first appeared. It was the heavy

make-up that made her seem older
> pancaked
> exquisite expensive
> ex a tube

'Will he be long?' she asked. 'It's just that I've come over here specially, you know.' She smiled
> falsely

'Perhaps I should introduce myself. I'm Barbara Gilmour. Dougie and I are old friends. Perhaps he might have mentioned me.'

She held out a small soft hand which Helen shook
> weakly
> the fingers hardly bending
> gripless
> should be kissed

'My name's Helen,' she replied. 'Douglas and I are new friends. And I dont know how long he will be.'

Barbara Gilmour smiled again. 'Eh... heh', she breathed. 'Yes...'

For a moment, they looked at each other, then Helen stepped back and opened the door. 'You'd better come in, then.'

'If it's not inconvenient. I dont want to be in your way.'
> telling
> tao

Barbara stepped over the threshold. Immediately she pointed to the bike. 'Why that was Hugh's, wasnt it? I remember it very well. Oh dear, poor Hugh.'
> words flurried
> space not given for reply
> pre-empting reaction
> but the wheel's off

Helen only nodded slowly. She led the way through to the lounge. Barbara followed her
> scanning everything
> canny eye

'I must say, Dougie has got this looking really nice. A little cluttered, but then he always was a hoarder.' She spun around on her not too high heel as she spoke, looking carefully about the room.

Helen sat down on her favourite chair that
> envelopes
> supports

A Day at the Office

the size of me

Barbara took one more eyesful of her, then sat on the sofa. She spread her arm out over its back until the whole of the seat seemed to be her own. 'Yes, very nice,' she repeated.

'Although I must say I'm a little surprised to find you here, Helen. No one mentioned you when they told me about this place.'

no one
which one
designed to cause fear
of the unknown one
best defence to dodge
the question

'Oh I'm not part of the furnishings, so it's hardly likely he would.' She flicked a quick smile over her face, then killed it just as quick

good at that
snarling

'Ah!' Barbara nodded slowly, then sighed

besooms prominently displayed
heaves

'Yes, this is quite a transformation for Dougie. The last time I was home, which is what, three years ago, he was still living with his mother.'

She paused, waited her moment. 'You've met Frances, of course?'

Oh she is a clever one at these games.

Helen sniggered. 'A pleasure in store,' she said. Barbara smacked her lips and tapped her toe on the polished pine floor, then sighed, watching

look down up over round
circling
stalking the prey
tiger lily

'I hope you dont mind me asking, but are you and Dougie, em…?

'What, playmates?'

Barbara laughed. 'Well, yes?'

Helen stood up without answering. She went over to the baby grand, where a bottle of whisky stood unopened, with glasses, on an empty tray. She lifted it up by the neck and showed it Barbara, who raised her eyebrows

silently

ask the question
let her interpret my tongue

'Well I dont usually drink during the day.'

Helen urged her. 'There's some soda here and ice in the fridge.'

'Well, since you put it like that, I think I will.'

Helen went to the kitchen to get the ice

so this is Douglas' world
seems like fun
very nice cosy people
if this Barbara was anything to go by

Huh. She got the ice out and put two cubes in each glass. When she went back to the lounge, Barbara had taken her furs off and was gazing out the window

eye
languid
a
cast
she

'Scotland. Dear old Escocia. Yes,' she said, 'It is nice here. I'm surprised, you know. When Douglas told me he was living in Blacklands, I thought, what? That ghetto! But he said that it was all being tidied up and he's right. It's really rather nice round here.'

really rather
relatively speaking
nice

Helen put in a good measure of whisky and filled it to the top with soda. Barbara seemed to like the look of it. She held up her glass and Helen clinked hers against it. 'To new friendships!' Barbara half sang out. Helen said 'Yes,' but

a bit premature
tempting fate with trust

They went back to their seats. Barbara caught Helen's eye and gave her a smile of melting intensity

this parade
so pointless
thinking
what was she thinking?
never just a social call
with such a pregnant silence

'So,' Barbara said, 'This is very nice.'

'Yes. You said so before.'

Barbara leaned forward. 'Come on now, Helen, you can

A Day at the Office

relax with me. I'm just an old friend. I've known Douglas since we were children. My mother and his were schoolfriends. I'm not trying to pry. I just want to be friends.'
She waited for Helen's response
but it will not materialise

'You see, I've been away for a long time. I was an air hostess with Pan-Am, met an American, we married and for the last four years, I've been living in Miami. But now we've split up and I'm back home again, it's difficult for me. I dont have many friends left here. Most of them have either moved away or we've just lost touch.'
that emphasis
the physical

She raised her glass and took another sip. She was still leaning forward trying to get inside Helen's confidence
worming not boring

Helen sniffed. 'That's odd, you know, I left my husband a few months ago.'

'Really! You seem so young.'

'I am young, I married young.' Barbara was waiting for further information. Helen took another drink
sweet sour hot

'I'm not trying to be nosey,' Barbara coaxed, 'But did you leave him for Douglas?'
the nerve
but
hold it
ruffle not

'No. It was before I met Douglas. I'd just had enough, you know.'

She stood up and went over to the piano to get another drink. Barbara leaned back in her seat as she passed.

'Yes, yes, I do know,' she answered. 'It's hard, living with a man. No matter how well you think you know them, they've always got some little secret up their sleeves.' She smiled mischievously.
lips tight

'I think they must be genetically incapable of real honesty.'

Helen laughed. 'It wasnt that with me. He just liked to hit me.'

'Jealous?'
was it?

'Maybe, though I dont know why. I gave him no reason to be.'

'Well, if you dont mind me saying so, you're a very attractive girl. Not that you advertise it. You simply are. Naturally.'
the faint praise
damns

Helen gave her a glare. 'Come off it. That's not reason enough to punch someone.' She held the open bottle up to Barbara, who rose and passed her glass over.

'Who said anything about reason, dear? There's nothing reasonable about jealousy.' She laughed to herself, a short nervous sound.

'God, I wish I'd been able to stir something equivalent in Danny. He was about as passionate as a terrapin.'
mutant hero
ninja not geisha

This time it was Helen who made the toast, with her glass raised.
with diffidence

'To past husbands, wherever they may be,' she said, and Barbara took up the sentiment. 'And long may they pay the alimony,' she added.

'I wouldnt take it,' Helen said.

Barbara's mouth curled up into a cunning grin. 'Oh I will. You bet I will. Every cent I can get out of the little bastard. He owes me something for all the time I wasted on him.'

And then she laughed, loudly, and peeped at Helen over the top of her glasses
mirthless

For a moment Helen thought it was a joke. She began to snigger. But the woman was serious
no doubt about it
every cent she had said
every cent was what she meant

Helen drained her glass and put it down by the whisky bottle
nice people were they
nice cosy people
there was something new here
a new kind of hardness
a kind of shiny tv mini series mentality at work

Barbara put down her glass too.

'Well,' she said, 'I'm sorry to say I must leave you, much as

I'd love to wait and see Douglas. I was really fascinated when I heard he was opening a gallery. I was hoping he might show me around.'

Shrugging, Helen stood up.

'There isnt much to see yet. He's always having to go zooming off somewhere, instead of getting on with it. Antiques. You probably know.'

'Yes, yes, of course.' She crossed to the sofa and picked up her coat. As she slipped it over her shoulder, she turned to Helen again. 'He always did have an eye for a pretty thing.'

catty

Helen ignored it. 'Why dont you give him a ring sometime, arrange a time. Maybe if you show an interest, you'll get him moving.'

far away

'Yes, I will. And I have enjoyed our wee chat, Helen. So nice to meet you. I hope we will be seeing more of each other. It's rather lonely being back here again, you know, after so long in America. Anyway, I must be off.'

Helen watched her go, across the street and into a BMW parked on the other side

it's funny
to think that people exist
you've invented
years before
but
it's work I do
and I must get ready

She went out of the lounge and into Douglas' bedroom. Her clothes and all her jewelry, her make-up, most of the things that she considered hers were in his flat now. Her own small flat upstairs was empty. But she liked to know that it was there, that she was paying rent for it and could use it as a bolthole if a time ever came when she thought it was necessary. Perhaps the wheel of fortune had turned and she was on the up slope, but wheels could turn, did turn, she knew. It was inevitable. So for the moment, work came first.

As she dressed, Helen felt a headache begin to nag at her

the world closing in
pressing on the skull
grave gravity and air in motion
the semi-circular canals

aswirl

She swallowed a couple of painkillers with a mouth of water. Then as she was leaving the flat, the telltale back pains started and she recognised what it was that was happening. The rain was quite heavy now. She had to run down the street to the bus stop.

out here
alone
the world reaches in
into my heart
Mrs King's flat there
blood-stained maybe
no sanctuary
no one
no wall between
the real and the dream

1530

      the dark dim
     has no date in here
      the office floor
    buoyed up with capital
     floats motionless
  as we modulate perfection
     in fluorescent strips
  maintain our concentration
    resist the tricks of time
    see each hidden card
     before it's played
  and scent the rabbit waiting
    up the wizards sleeve
         yet
    those paper figures
  edging closer to the time
  where I will meet and wrestle
    their accounted tally
    are strong enough
      to make me
      want to be
      the victim
of some other circumstance
  oh i ray something's
      happening
I'm in the centre of it at last
      herewith

This Shaw guy driving quickly through the city, heading back over the river, towards the south side. He took a sharp right at Blacklands Cross
              near here once
              passed through

Ray sat back to enjoy the magical mystery tour. It wasnt far before Shaw pulled the Toyota up outside a block of flats.

  –Come on, Shaw said as he got out, still grinning, and went up to the main door, which he opened. Ray followed him in, noticing how clean the close was, the daylight showed the tiles were gleaming green and brown and orange and white
            even the mosaic patterned
              on the floor shines

Shaw led the way up the stairs onto a landing lined with green plants.
Some winter bulbs   hyacinths?   blooming.
He stopped in front of the second door and opened it with a key picked out from a bunch.

–This used to be my girlfriend's flat. Well not so much a flat as a bedsit. Some of her things are still up here, but if you're interested in it, it wont take long to sort things out.

Inside a small hallway were two more doors
wonderland unfolding
Shaw led the way into a room which looked out over the front of the building onto the street. The window was covered with a cane blind, but you could see through. There was a small couch, a chair and some shelving in an alcove with some books and tapes and stuff like that. Ray glanced over the titles. There was a copy of *The Queen is Dead*
. a woman of taste
liztwo
The room smelled as if it had been recently painted. Ray went over to look out through the window. Shaw pulled up the blind.

–Good view he said. Shaw was standing beside him. In a gap site between the buildings, you could see the bulk of Torry Hill and just a glimpse of the river where it became the firth.

–Yes it is, Shaw muttered, –Though I tend to take it for granted. He turned away to a small closet off the main room.

– The bed is in here, he said. –There isnt really space for anything else.

– Then over here, he crossed the room, –This door takes you out to the shared facilities. Kitchen, with a washing machine, bathroom.

Ray stood in the doorway looking from one room into the next
doors
rooms
a door was finally opening
for
i ray
– Oh one thing, Shaw said, –The woman across the landing from you, she can be a bit fussy, especially about people leaving unwashed dishes, that sort of thing. But she's quite

pleasant really. Divorcee, works in a bank. Then upstairs from you again, there's five engineering students. They're a quiet bunch for students. Must be these austere times we live in
                    this is not real
                    isnt it happening
–Where's the catch?
                    to me
Shaw chuckled. –There isnt one, Ray. At least not from my side. The rent is £40 per week, though if you're unemployed, I dont suppose there will be a problem with that. I'll get you a copy of the lease for the Housing Department. You know about all that, I presume
                    oh i nod
–Normally I'd ask for a deposit. But I've got a feeling that you and I will get on well. There may be the odd occasion when I'll need you to do some work for me. Moving things about, you know
                    couriering
                    careering
                    it doesnt matter
                    whatever
                    i agree
– So what do you think, interested?
                    i want to say
                    something clever
                    but
–I want it
                    but
Shaw laughed loudly. –Good. How about we go downstairs and I'll show you where I live? I want you, you know, to feel at ease here
                    lead me to it
He led the way down to the flat on the ground floor. The hall was large and dark but full of bits and pieces. He opened the door into a sunny spacey room
                    a clutter of beautiful things
                    art books
                    ornaments
                    paintings standing against a wall
As he nosed about Ray realised it wasnt as chaotic as it first appeared. In fact the chaos could have been deliberate. Pieces of stained glass, like picture fragments out of a church window, were hung from the ceiling in exactly the spot that

would show them off
> as ordered disorder

In the middle of the room was a baby grand piano and underneath it were enough shoes to foot an army, all neatly set out pairs, side by side. It was a queer mix of finished order and things half done. The more he looked around the more caught his eye. At the far side of the room was a giant bed covered in a brightly coloured patchwork quilt, with mirrors, satin and velvet shapes. An oak dresser, superbly carved, stood against one wall, while opposite it in the window bay was an arrangement of tall, thin-legged tables, supporting some huge healthy looking plants with patterned leaves. Shelves in an alcove were stacked with little bits and pieces. A small stuffed alligator or crocodile poked its head down from the wall above his head. It was too much
> like some exotic bird
> or tropical flower fairy

–This place is incredible, Ray said at last. –Really incredible.

Shaw clucked his funny laugh. –Most of it's stock from the shop. I cleared everything out a few weeks ago ready for a refurbishing job downstairs. The antique shop as it then was. These pieces needed a safe home for a while. And anyway I love them, I'm a bit of a hoarder, always have been. I hate selling the pieces I like.

He went to the window and produced from behind the curtain a folding screen with some Japanese or Chinese painting on it, a waterfall scene with birds flying over the abyss. He set the screen between the piano and the street outside.

–Discretion, you know what I mean I hope, he winked
> oh i nod
> in these riches
> among things and money
> agreeable

Standing alongside the piano, he took a small shiny box and a packet of Camels out of his pocket, and started the rolling on the piano top.

–It's like a museum in here. Or maybe an art gallery, Ray muttered, moving around the room examining first this then that. There was so much to study
> small things
> jewelled things

> big things
> silver things
> thing things

–Some of it isnt all it seems, Shaw said. –For instance that vase at your side? It was broken when I bought it. If you look carefully you'll see where on the neck. I would hate to think what it would have fetched if it had been perfect. The fact it was broken doesnt bother me though. It's not the idea of the object being pure I'm interested in. It's the way they travel through time.

> time travel too?
> who are you?

Ray could only wag his head lamely, not shaking it or nodding it. Shaw came over and offered him the smoke to light. Ray drew back.

–No it's alright, on you go, he said, but he was offered it again.

–Sit down, relax

> dont do it

Ray located a chair and took a light from Shaw's hand. The taste was the one familiar thing in the whole room. He sucked in the smoke greedily while Shaw went over and put on some music on the deck.

> Mozart or something
> opera maybe
> combination of the sound
> the speed of all that's happening
> seems to sharpen senses

Ray looked at Shaw standing there smiling at him and for the first time seemed to see him clearly, there in his own world among his many possessions. His skin was so soft and unblemished, his hair so soft and blond, his eyes excited like a wee boy's

> it's that look
> like a kid
> that's a what I like
> not his show-off

He seemed as if he was charmed with a sureness of himself

> Is this what it is
> to have wealth?
> another toke
> pass it
> question

—Where did you get this stuff?
Shaw frowned. —I though you'd know never to ask a dealer where it comes from.
—No, no I dont mean the smoke. I mean all this stuff here. I mean I know you said it came from the shop, but it must have come from somewhere before that.
Shaw considered for a while as he smoked. Finally, after about three minutes, he said —That's an intriguing question. Things come to me. I dont feel as if I actually go out and collect them. And it isnt anything to do with owning them
own oh?
As he spoke, his eyes moved around the room
like he was in a church
looking at a lot of holy relics
like maybe they could hear him when he spoke
and would tell God what he said
—You know, Ray, sometimes I think that these things, these inanimate objects, have souls of some kind. Do you believe in the existence of souls?
Ray shrugged. —I dunno. I never really thought about it before.
—It's as if they took some part of their creator's soul. Perhaps in the way that we all partake of some universal soul. Or perhaps it's their creator's mark, their fingerprint that does the trick. A tiny part of their maker's spirit. Like us and God maybe?
maybe no
A marker on a journey through spacetime, maybe powerless in itself, but capable of activating change in the life of anyone who really looks at them?
i'm no sure what you're on about
sounds like a lot of bull
bermuda triangle curse of the pharoah UFO bull
—Sceptical? I dont really blame you. I suppose what I'm trying to say is that collecting things isnt really that different from the way people pick each other out in a crowd. Like you and I, brought here by coincidence.
—Right? But then people can become catalytic in each others lives from just that kind of beginning
i'm struggling
cataclytic?
—Well perhaps not catalytic. But it's along those lines. These

things, they use me, you know, as I use them. These are my mandalas, my icons. Through them I get access to mysteries and magic I cant even dream of without them. A journey through space time. Real magic that. And I in turn care for them, preserve their physical existence. Are you with me?

in spirit man
but oh the flesh
sweak

–Magic is all about time and space, right? If you take it in its simplest form, or in its slowest form, the kind of trickery a cabaret act deals in, if you slow the movement down enough and get the camera at the right angle, chances are you'll be able to see the thing disappear or appear or whatever it does. You might not be able to see where the thing comes from or where it ends up but you'll see it move. Because it doesnt just disappear. The whole idea of what it does is relative to how observant the human eye is and how quick the thing moves.

Intrigued, as much by Shaw's performance as by his words, Ray listened.

–Now you take this thing here.

He tapped the piano top. –No so-called magician on the cabaret circuit makes these things disappear up his sleeve. Well not that I know of anyway. But a hypnotist could convince, by delaying the signal from your eye to your brain, by messing up your normal pattern of observation

see?

–Now what you do when you walk into this room is observe, right? The things around seem to be here. But if you had walked into this room even six months ago, very few of these things would have been here. They would have been down below in the shop. But if you had been hypnotised from the time of entering the room until now, you would have thought, on wakening, that these things had appeared here by magic. Out of nowhere, suddenly into this room. I would have had to explain to you that you had been asleep.

He was pacing out a careful track on the carpet, looking down at each potential step as he was taking it, then came to an abrupt stop in front of Ray.

–That's the magic of it. How things come to be where they are. How they're moved about by hands you never see. If you're in on the trick from the beginning, there's no magic.

Understand?
>   æ i e o u
>   no not right
>   not that way

Ray could not hold back his laughter. All he could think of was how this guy looked like a loonie pacing up and down in a cosy padded cell with nothing to do but think up daft ideas. When he heard Ray's laugh, Shaw's face looked hurt for a second, then he began to laugh himself.

–Sorry sorry, Ray. I dont know where I get these thoughts from. Sometimes my tongue seems to connect straight to my brain. I'm sorry for rambling on
>   say something nice
>   why say it again

–No it's interesting, honest.

–How did I get started on all that anyway?

They both sat for a minute trying to remember
>   flashback
>   where does it come from?
>   never ask
>   not that
>   it's souls

–Souls, Ray answered. –You were talking about souls.

Shaw laughed again. –Yes, that was it! But his humour didnt last long. He turned away as a sort of heavy troubled look came to his face. He sat down on the bed and then after a moment looked up at the wall above Ray's head.

–Well maybe they do at that.

Ray twisted round and looked above him. Staring down from the picture rail was a mask that he hadnt noticed earlier. It was startling
>   how did i miss it
>   horror cold

shocking, the face so thin and long with areas of bright white and black separated by studded lines of something shiny, like mother of pearl
>   i wouldnt change you for another girl

The eyes were close together and the nose was sharp like the point of a spear. At the top of an angular forehead, wisps of knotted string or cord were swept back like hair from the face. But the mouth was the real shocker. Though it was small, it was slightly open, as if it was ready to talk

A Day at the Office

or bite or kiss

and inside you could see row upon row of tiny white pointed teeth, like shark's teeth if they'd been bigger

how did i no see it?

–Yes especially him, Shaw said. –Though I do know how he got here. My grandfather brought him back from New Guinea. It's illegal now, to take any tribal art like that out of the country. It's strange but I've always had the feeling that he's never really been happy in our family. Even in this room, he keeps roaming around like a caged animal. We are no doubt far too civilised for him

or uncivilised

Ray stared at the mask for a long time.

does he mean that he believes this thing actually moves around?

–So you reckon he has a soul, this guy?

Shaw frowned. – For want of a better word, yes.

–And you think that these souls, for want of a better word, they're attracted to you and you dont really collect them?

Shaw got up and went over to a shelf in an alcove. On it was a collection of pipes. He pulled out a small brass one and began to fill it.

–Well I suppose I do collect them in the sense that I bring them together in a certain time space, you know, that I give them house room.

Ray grinned. – But do you buy them?

heh yeah

The stress he put on the word buy seemed to surprise Shaw. He edged further away behind the piano

hiding?

–Money doesnt really come into it for me, though I suppose it is a consideration for most collectors.

He strode over to Ray with the stocked pipe, then held up a lighter with his thumb on the wheel of it ready to flash the flame. Ray hesitated, he wasnt really happy with Shaw's answer.

cmoan

–I'll tell you when it comes into it, he said, –It comes into it when you've no got it, then sucked the pipe alight

heh yeah

Shaw pulled the lighter away.

–I've heard that one before, he said, and you're probably

right as far as capital goes, but this is different. These are things, not money. Some of the pieces I value most highly cost me next to nothing.
 —But not exactly nothing?
 —Some of them.
aye presents no doubt
from other rich folk
 Ray smiled, unconvinced. — So you reckon things would come to me, even though I've got no money?
 Not expecting an answer right away, he put the pipe in his mouth and relit it himself. The strength of the toke hit Ray in the back of the throat but he wouldnt allow himself to cough.
 —Yes, Shaw said. I don't see why not. Do you?
 Ray handed him the pipe back. Shaw frowned, took it and turned away. He didnt inhale immediately, but used the stem of the pipe as a pointer, like a teacher lecturing a pupil.
 —But they may not be the same things as would come to me or anybody else for that matter
crap
 Ray grinned. —I suppose the things that would come to me would cost less though.
 This time it was Shaw who nearly broke out coughing. He tapped the bowl of the pipe, emptied its contents into an ashtray and began refilling it.
 Ray's head was reeling but
i want more
 Shaw chuckled. —You've got to pick your luck, he said.
 —A tramp can find a fortune if he's in the right place in the right time.
 Ray coughed. —Aye and a dog can find the World Cup but that doesnt mean to say he gets to keep it.
 Shaw burst into a fit of laughter. —You're bitter, Ray, I like that. I've never had much of a sweet tooth myself. Much better to expect nothing, no doubt, that way everything's a bonus
meaning what
that you're the one that's got
the goods to give
 —Things will come, Ray, Shaw said, smiling now
look says
is that a promise?
 —You've got to believe.
 Ray felt himself to be

> a cynic
> am i ray
> cynical
> hope less?

—Aye, well, it's kind of the way I want to be, you know, I want to believe that stuff about magic and souls and stuff, but
> how to say this it

—You were born into this, were you no?

—An accident of birth?

—Aye that's it. You can spread it round a bit, you know, but that choice isnt open to me, see? It's not enough to pick your luck like you say, it's picked for you.

Shaw was nodding, he was agreeing
> this bastard knows i'm right
> and he's laughing
> cos the games his

—Maybe you could steal some, Ray.

—Steal some what?

—Luck. Be the Robin Hood of Fate. Steal from the lucky and give it to the unlucky
> oh i it's fine for you to laugh
> but give me a gun man
> i'll have yours

Ray said nothing. He realised the game was up
> let the edge blunt
> no win
> no claims
> they own the pond

Shaw tapped the pipe and turned away. It was
> the time has come to go
> but
> i ray'll be
> back
> wait an see

—Listen, I better get moving.

—Moving in?
> he's got it to give
> an i want to get it
> but i dont want to take it from him

—Are you sure, about the bedsit, I mean?

—You've seen it, if you want it, it's yours
> if i take it
> he takes me

—Ok.

1559

THE MASK I WAS ONCE FOLLOWS ME
AROUND
THOUGHTS OF OLD FRIENDS
OLD BOOKS OLD SONGS
OLD FRIENDS
BUD OPEN AT THE SLIGHTEST NUDGE
AND THERE I SULK
BEFORE I SIGNED THE CONTRACT
SAYING PLAINLY WITH MY STANCE
give me your suit
i have ambition
give me your shoes I'll fill em
A SALARY'S NOT HARD TO SPEND
WHEN THERE'S REPAYMENTS
ON THE MORTAGE
ON THE CAR LOAN
AND THE PLASTIC
WHEN THERE'S AN EMPTY HOUSE
AND LIFE TO PACK
oh yes it's true
there's always someone
waiting for your shoes as you yourself once waited
for another's
and you are but connecting
two together

like this something about Ray that brought to Douglas mind his brother
        a mix of elements maybe
        lines of the hand
        configuration of the planets

As he went down the steps to the shop in the basement, he caught sight of Hugh's initials set firm in the concrete, written with a small boy's Jupiter finger many years ago. It was when they were there with their father, when the shop was being boarded over and the broken drain outside the basement door was repaired. It was like a link to the living line
        of trees along the path

The memory stirs
        they must have been showing those black buds
        like the chrysalises of butterflies

A Day at the Office

                    it was at that time of the year
                    the winter skin unfolds to green
                    the tarmac must have carried tracks
                        of early morning moisture
                        the print of his bicycle tyres
                                between
              the corporation football pitches to the north
            and the rubgy fields belonging to the High School
                    around the saddle of the bike
                        the coil of rope
            he would have pedalled up the hill to the tree
                    we knew from boyhood
                            where
                with bent nails and orange box plinth
                    we built the gang hut
                    he knew the ash tree well
            he would have seen that it had changed little
                since the time when we were boys
                    at least this is how I imagine it
                        I can never be sure
                        I cant really imagine it
                though the power of it imagines me
            there are so many questions I cant answer
                            where
                        did he get the rope?
                            why
                did he do it in the early morning?
                        had he been
                        up all night?
                            or
                            had he
            woken to the knowledge that it was time?
            I know he took money without giving back
                        he stole from me
                though I never looked on it as theft
                        his intentions were good
                    I could see it hurt his pride
                        to let us down like that
                        I didnt know how bad
            I wonder most of all about the planning
                        the intricate steps
                            he had to
                    get the rope from somewhere
                        fix it on the bike
                    choose the route to the park
                        choose the tree
            always closing in on the moment in his mind
                when he would make the noose

           the determination necessary
                 I cant imagine
                to tie the rope
         to put the thing around his neck,
                    to jump
                    or slip
                   down down
        a last swinging glimpse of wet earth
       a crocus poking out of a crack in the grass

           I took a poppy to the graveside
                But I didnt drop it in
          not while those black crows watched
                   It was raining
             and I couldnt wait to get away
         I just squashed it in the palm of my hand
              the half-formed seed pod
                  cool like plastic
             the petals velveteen and moist
                  dying on my skin
              the suits were all so stiff
             I felt their grief was stiff as well
            in the silence that she split with sobs
           I saw how little she really understood
              I took the bicycle home with me
                   but never use it
      instead it just stands against the wall in my hall
               I look at it as I go out
                and touch it sometimes
                   when I come in
                        yes
                      mother
                let me tell you plain
                   pain we share
                        yet
                     we must
                   but let it go
                     for death
                      to die
     here was this place, this shop, these flats, this was the place
                where Hugh had lived
                   chosen to die
                left the scraps of life
                   for me to rake
                        like
                   burning embers
       that could never be used to rekindle the fire
               just ash in the shape of coals

> one poke for
> disintegration
> dust every wherewithal

Long ago Douglas knew that his brother had chosen his way, this tao. Even though he had tried to shut the knowledge out, then desperately, through guilt, he tried to sway him. To get him making, doing, being something other than a junkie. Even when he gave up trying, he kept on trying, hoping to edge him towards some positive pole that might exert a pull he couldnt.

He thought at least he would have some time, that Hugh would let the needle take its trick, pricking out the patterns, injecting into the life stream a course of euphoric death

> but what I didnt realise is
> it was a way
> a tao
> valid in negation
> the craziest most extreme balancing act of all
> that self-induced suffering
> but in that suffering
> something else occurs
> something almost spiritual
> impure yes, rotting away
> but a glimpse of something
> some otherness

There was the time he took Mother's Peploe and sold it for next to nothing. That was when she withdrew from the arena. He was beyond her then, he had lost faith in art and its intrinsic value, therefore life and its intrinsic value. There could be no forgiveness. Douglas went to see him

> yes it was here in this building
> here when it was Hugh's
> before I inherited it
> the whole hellhole
> we shared a spliff
> drank Highland Park
> dad's favourite

He relaxed. Douglas could see that he was fighting back again, but he was making no predictions about kicking it for ever. He said

> he said
> people dont realise
> but junkies are often really aware
> sensitive people who just cant bear the bleakness they see

in suffering, in martyrdom, it is possible to attain enlightenment and transcend
> put the maggot that falls
> from the hole in your shoulder back
> poor maggot

He said you see these junkie kids on television being interviewed by some faceless extension of the social conscience, these kids dont come over as fools, in their way they're wise, they've tasted poison, theyve known death in life, they're old at fourteen. He said sure you die but what kind of gauge is time anyway, when it's consciousness we're measuring. He said I'd give up twenty years to really know, really know what it is to be at peace
> rest in peace
> he said
> it's the shortest cut of all, kid brother
> a menace to society?
> that's rich

He said it's all to do with framing the question. A drug has no power to get inside the body. People take drugs, drugs dont take people. The question is why? What is it about life that makes them do it? Inability to cope with reality? But what's reality?
> he said reality varies
> drugs are real
> drug realities are real
> but not like real reality

He said take alcohol, the western ritual, you drink at the birth, and the marriage and the death. You drink at your business conference, at your night out
> he said for drugs
> substitute wealth
> the only high better than getting high
> is knowing you can afford to get high whenever you want to

Hugh said people cant. External forces dictate, not just money, but responsibility to others, we cant just cut off into our own reality.
> we've got to understand other people's viewpoint
> even fascists
> cause it's there in us all
> that dictatorial voice
> self discipline
> which is ok for the self, man
> but when you start to press it on other people

A Day at the Office

                    when you start sticking folk in fucking ovens
                            people you've never even met
                                    jesus
                                   he said
                                    Jesus
That was the last time Douglas saw him alive. It was a good time
                                    close
He was glad he spent it with him, he was glad that he had gone there and listened to what he had to say. When he left that night he had the feeling that there was some hope that Hugh was working his way free of it. All that talk about drugs, that was new, it was as if he was trying desperately to objectivise his addiction so that he could overcome it
                          which he did I suppose
                                 in one way
But the waste of that mind and that life. What it might have offered to Douglas in terms of accumulated wisdom, that loss sickened him. Hugh had a really peculiar way of looking at the world, but somehow it made sense. It all made sense. And he could make music, he could write, he could paint, he had these abilities
                           far in excess of mine
                           that story for instance
                       the one he showed me that night
                              it had something
                         ok it was a real down mood
                                    but
                              when I read it
                                  ohhhhhh
The old man had been hanging from the edge of his bed with his head just touching the floor. When he moved he did so with the metamorphic suddenness of a small lizard, and took a stub of pencil from the folds of the coarse blanket covering the mattress. He began writing on the paper they had provided.

'*I have been in this place for so long that I can no longer resist my guilt. Daily I relive the moments of decision and realise that I was neither right nor wrong. Time has ceased to matter. When I was first brought here, I counted the days as if calculating the quantity of wrong done to me. Now I do not care for time, if I am ever released, it will be too soon and for all the wrong reasons. I have accepted this existence.*

'The only gulf into which we can fall is God's hands. This phrase keeps recurring in my mind from some source which I cannot identify. I have no books or library here to consult. Yet this phrase has assumed great significance for me. I fall endlessly. I now practise hanging upside down from my bed, like Odin awaiting enlightenment. At first I was afraid that I might collide with some bottom – I could still see my past life like a light above – but when I had been falling so long as to extinguish this, the thought of there ever being any kind of bottom seemed ridiculous. I am suspended in a state of perpetual gravitational pull, ever falling never fallen.'

He hesitates, then lays the pencil down. At his feet is a pile of similarly scribbled pages, each with the same tight handwriting at one end of the paper only. He places this most recent one on top of the others carefully. He had not yet fully accepted the guilt, though he was close to doing so now. Yet no matter how many times he tried to write the words he sensed they wanted, he would always abandon certainty and resort to supposition. They knew this and so they kept him here, without daylight, human association, time. Nothing but the voice from the loudspeaker in the centre of the ceiling out of reach. He lies with his feet on his bed, tucked under the cylindrical metal bar at its head, with his own head hanging down to the floor. His body twists awkwardly. The pain in his abdominal muscle provides a variance of sensation, almost welcome in this place where homogeneity ruled. His cell was a perfect cube of blankness, without window, without door. A frustrating symmetry broken only by the recess which held the lift that brought his food and removed his waste. He knew there had to be a door but had failed to discover which of the panels it was. All around this strange grey material that seemed to absorb dust. What light he saw seemed to glow from the panels.

He could not remember being brought here, although the feeling of being powerless to resist still haunted him. His memory of arrest, if arrested he had been, was gone. But the guilt remains. They ensure this by means of the sleeptalk. They waited till his resistance was lowest. Each time he tried to sleep, they kept waking him with loud noises. Then when he could not be stirred at all, the guilt talk began. He knew what

A Day at the Office

it was they wanted. Why else would they have sent him the paper?

Names, they wanted the names of his so called conspirators. Symbols, keys perhaps, that they could use against him. But the only clear memory was that of the guilt. In their attempts to extract from him what they wanted, they had accentuated this sense till all others were lost. Thus they had made an error which could not be rectified and were bound to torture him until he died. If he was not already dead, in which case there would be no end to torture. If he could have remembered, he would have given them names, any names, he would have invented them. But he could not. He had even forgotten his own.

He lifts his head from the hanging position and stretches out on the bare mattress. He wonders how old he is. His hands were bony and the skin was taut. All lines had been erased, line of life, line of heart, line of head, line of Saturn, line of Apollo, gone like his fingerprints. If he plucked hair from his head, it was white.

Then in an instant he was free. One moment there was no exit, the next there was. The process happened silently, with no torrent from his subconscious. He rose up and passed through the space which had opened. He walks slowly along a corridor made of the same grey white material. He had the feeling that he was walking up a slight incline but it was so slight that he could not be sure. Perhaps there were slow curves that changed his direction but no corners. Only the corridor. His feet seemed cushioned by the flooring. After a while he noticed that the corridor had grown wider. It must have happened very slowly over a number of metres. When he stretched his arms out wide, he could not touch the sides. Above his head the ceiling was well out of reach. Step by step he was gaining space, widening the restriction.

Then he was stung by a fear. What if this was taking him nowhere? What if it led into another cell? He stopped. The corridor tilted downwards. They wanted him to walk now, they were making it hard for him to stop. Soon he might be careering downwards, with nothing to hold on to. The corridor was so wide now that even if he had lain down and tried to wedge himself between the walls it would have been futile.

He had no choice but to go on. The floor began to level again. They were monitoring his progress.

He reached an end panel. As he stood before it, expecting a space to appear before him, another grey white panel appeared behind and he was trapped inside a space so small that he began to suck at the air for fear of losing breath. The wide walls closed about him till he was upright in a space no bigger than a coffin.

Then the ceiling dematerialised and he looked up to see a light of dazzling white above, like an equatorial sun at noon. He began swaying from wall to wall, unable to speak out or cry. He had the sensation of being transported up, as in a lift shaft, towards the light. He began to cry then, but as the first tear appeared, the coffin evaporated as one and he could see nothing. The light swamped all. He fell to his knees and waited. The light above began to dull.

A slow red grew as the sun died, till it swelled about him, emanating from every atom. The air became heavier and moist. If he moved, it was as if he pushed against something restrictive, but comforting. He ceased breathing. There seemed to be no need. Something was sheltering him. He was safe.

A heavy echoing beat filled him, pulsing from the redness. The old man felt himself become very small, vulnerable and naked. He curled up into a tiny ball of flesh, tucking his knees under his chin, turning slowly in the heaviness. He needed nothing. He knew they had never existed, nor had his prison. These phantoms were merely creations of his old age, the limits of his endurance, the end of movement and imagining. But now he was still and thought no more. He would grow. His tiny fingers would form and his nostrils would curve like the shell of snail, filled with mucus till the time came. The time would come.

He was growing again. He was swelling and growing. The heartbeat set the rhythm, not his. Pulsing in the glow there was a sound of an irregular nature, a fluid gurgling, sometimes staccato chattering. This too was comforting. The time would come for air and hunger.

I made the mistake that night

A Day at the Office

                      I thought
this story was the beginning of something new
       a worldly adventure for Hugh
               a writer
       another cause to replace
         the junkie in him
           he had been
           active once
I thought maybe he would be again
            I was wrong
          this was not
           a beginning
        this was the end
and the last will and testament
            named me
        I am his heir
          to the shop
         to the sorrow
           the care
         why should I
care about this Ray? Why should he help him, other than that they had met in this fortuitous way and that there was something about him that inexplicably brought his dead brother closer to him
             strength
perhaps, an inner strength that came from having nothing much to lose, that was remote enough from ego to allow it to perform its magic without one's temper interfering, so that its hands were not afraid to grip the jaws of even lions
              while I
          despite the all
             it all
      am hanging upside down
              still

1640
you've had long enough
to think about it
JUST SIGN HERE
TAKE THE BOTTOM COPY
you know you really need this
dont you
YOU REALISE THERE'S NOTHING
BUT THIS FOR YOU
same place same time tomorrow
NO FIDDLING DONT BE LATE
the work rote
starts for Helenme and

by the time she got to the casino, it was pouring. She went to the staff locker room and changed into the short black skirt and frilly white blouse she was obliged to wear. She hated the clothes

> the material
> the hem line
> the whole look
> of the uniform
> what it represented
> the servant

She had to begin clearing her tables as soon as she went in. The previous shift had already gone and with them the tips. More people came in and sat down and it was fifteen minutes before she had the chance to take a breather by the Cona-coffee table in the still-room.

'Busy the night.' It was wee Annie. 'Want a fag?'

Helen took one.

'You're looking awful peaky, Helen. You feeling ok?'

Helen nodded. 'I'm alright. I've had a pretty hellish day.' Annie leant forward, curious. Helen felt obliged

> warm to talk about it
> to a distant familiar

'This old woman in the close next to ours was assaulted last night and there's been policemen poking about all day.'

Wee Annie's face fell into shock. 'Was it sexual?'

'I dont think so. The woman was about eighty.'

'Still, you'll need to watch. There might be a maniac on the loose.'

A Day at the Office

Helen didnt want to engage. She wanted to be
vacant there
in the still room
smell of coffee
slightly burnt
the ring's too hot
better
turn it down

Annie lit the cigarette she had given Helen. The smoking process protracted so that their confidence was established fully.

'So did you see anything then?'

'Where?'

'This old wife you said about.'

'What, blood, Annie?'
horror thirst
needs quenched
tabloid talk
at table talk

'Is she dead or what?'

'What.'

'What?'

'She's no dead she's what.'
wasted
wit

Annie was looking at her with her nose slightly wrinkled up, her eyes curiously screwed, but
unsure what is meant

'You said is she dead or what. I said what. It's a joke, Annie.'

'Oh!'
intoning
humourless
what do you want from me?

'I didnt get it ... '
i did
what does it say about you when you cant see a joke
or when your jokes fall flat and die

But that was it. The main topic of debate for the rest of the shift. Conducted in the usual manner, in fragmented episodes between kitchen and stillroom. And everybody had an opinion and some advice. The very hours they worked marked them out as targets, solitary women travelling home in the

middle of the night. A taxi home was no protection. Any one of the men at the tables might be waiting his chance
>   eyeing one of us up
>   following me home

Even the head waiter took an interest in the chat. But Helen started to get annoyed by all their questions – where did she live? What exactly happened? What kind of lock did she have on her door? It felt like an intrusion into private space, like the second policeman's visit. She knew it was well intentioned but she wished she had kept her mouth shut. Finally her temper snapped and she told the commis chef to mind his own business. But they all took this to be a sign that she was upset and became overly quiet and sympathetic
>   you cant win

The shift was busy. People kept streaming in, and she tried to concentrate on just getting through it, taking orders, carrying plates back and forward, laying cutlery, wiping and cleaning. She tried to do it all like it was a dance, to make it interesting, but she knew she was tired of it
>   five months is long enough
>   way too long
>   it got me out
>   got me money that was mine
>   that Colin couldnt hide
>   but now there is no point

Nobody stayed there long. It was too much graft for too little money. Consequently the restaurant was always in a shambles with folk who didnt really know what it was they were supposed to be doing. There were far too many part-timers cutting in for a night here a night there. Too many eaters
>   it is not a thing to be
>   not on the bottom rung
>   if you had the necessary poise
>   you had the choice
>   you could move upstairs, Helen
>   a hostess or a croupier
>   to the tables
>   the money is better

But she'd turned that down already and this was a dead end.

The casino wasnt as interesting as she thought it would be. It was just about money. If you didnt get excited about money,

A Day at the Office

you couldnt get excited about gambling. But there was something nevertheless about the air of the place, or perhaps the aura of the kind of person who went there.

Her dad had never been a gambler. He was a sportsman, a fisherman most of all. But her uncle Jimmy, he was a different story, a guy with a bet in every shop on every pay day. She could remember too the bingo wins her mum sometimes came home with. The unexpected change in fortunes. That was the drug

                    the rolling dice
                    the spinning wheel
                    not the way it landed
                    or the prize

but the anticipation

                    the race
                    the chase

When she started work there, she thought there would be some sort of person who would go gambling for that thrill alone, who wouldnt care about the money

                    romantic nonsense

She hadnt seen one yet. If a person was really after thrills they wouldnt be here, they'd be

                halfway up a glacier in Nepal
                  or playing chess
                      or
                    something

But people kept coming back, time after time, ready to give it a go. Maybe they did sometimes win. Maybe they enjoyed losing, or enjoyed not caring about losing. She had seen it now and again

                    but

it was cold in the restaurant, despite the efforts to keep out what was now the storm. Every time the door opened, a great gust of wind and drizzle blew in and the fan heaters up above it couldnt compete. Outside was worse

              thunder and lightning bolts
              watching through the window
              you could see the people
              going back and forth
              clowns on tightropes
              wobbling about with umbrellas
              hats taking off for the sky

She half expected to see a Mary Poppins flight before the day was out.

'Helen?'

She turned round. It was Stuart, wrapped in a huge trench coat, his head near disappeared under a furry Russian hat.

'Stuart!' she smiled. 'How did you know I was working here?'

'Douglas told me.' He seemed a bit down. His face was puffy and his eyelids looked heavy.

'Are you feeling ok? You look terrible.'

He grunted. 'I've had the flu. All last week, I was in my bed. It was hellish. Never saw a soul all week. Couldnt get out to the shops in the village. Worst week of my life.'

She took the pile of cutlery to the table.

'So what brings you into town then?'

'Civilisation,' he answered glumly. 'I want to see some people. How about me taking you out for something to eat?'

'I only just got here an hour ago. I'm not due a break for ages.'

'Could you not make up a story, get an hour off.'

'We're a bit short staffed.'

'I'm buying

> no reason not to
> could go
> sit down
> out of here
> what the hell

'What time is it now?'

He checked his watch. 'Half seven.'

'I suppose I could get off for a bit. The headwaiter and the chef are having some kind of conference till nine.'

'Drinking the sherry you mean.'

She laughed. 'You might be right.'

'Well are you coming?'

> okok
> nodok
> big strange brother man

'I'll just see if I can swop breaks with one of the others.'

The manager ok-ed it. She fetched her coat, and they headed out the side door and down the lane together. It was too wild a night to walk far, so they went into the first place they came to

> a small
> as-much-as-you-can-eat-for-your-money

A Day at the Office

wholefood restaurant. It was packed out. They had to wait for ages in the queue

legs
anache
wannasit
eat
drink

When they finally got to a table, she was exhausted. Stuart took off his Arctic gear and they sat down. Helen was hungry and had heaped her plate with various spoonfuls, but Stuart's was a much more modest helping. He didnt even seem hungry, just picked at it with a fork in his right hand, while she made

holes in the mountain

'I hear you've moved in with Douglas,' he said, then brought out a paper tissue and blew his nose loudly

trumpeteering

'Who told you that?' she said disinterestedly.

'He did.'

'Oh? I wonder why he would have said that when it isnt true.'

She went back to work on the food, trying to pretend she wasnt bothered. Stuart poked about in his portion of bean salad for a few moments, then put his fork down. She avoided asking what was the matter, just carried on eating. He blew his

nose trumpet again

'Damn this cold.'

'I thought you said it was the flu.'

'Flu, cold. What's the difference when you feel miserable.'

She stopped eating, took a drink from a glass of milk.

'You sure you should be out in this weather? You look terrible, you know. What is it they say, death warmed up? You're more like cold dead custard.'

Her voice wasnt as concerned as she intended it to sound. Instead, it went over like she was trying to get rid of him

scrape the custard off the plate
coffee?

Stuart shrugged, picked up his fork and made a feeble attempt at cutting a baked potato. The fork slipped and the tattie went spinning off the plate, landed on his lap. He picked it up and threw it back on the plate, then dumped his fork and knife down in a final gesture of irritation.

'I'm hungry, but I cant eat, know what I mean?'

'No,' she said, 'but if you really dont want that, I'll eat it.'
> he hardly touched it
> I'm starvin

'Go ahead.'

She lifted his plate and transferred all but the tattie onto hers. Stuart said nothing for a while, just sat looking round the restaurant, as if he expected everyone to be watching her. Then he lit a cigarette, and narrowed his eye to her cautiously.

'Are you sure you know what you're doing?'

She stopped, a fork of humus halfway to her mouth.

'I'm eating your dinner. What's the matter, do you think I'm liable to catch something?'
> not unlikely
> but I'm so incredibly hungry
> he hardly touched it

He pulled a face at her. 'Dont be such a brat.'

'You've got me with that one.' She gave him an I dont care smirk
> cleverer

'Forget it.' He leant away, sniffed, then blew his nose again.

'You know what I mean. Douglas and you. Are you sure it's such a good idea, Helen.'

'How's that?'

A man in soaking wet overcoat, balancing a heaped tray, tried to squeeze between Stuart and the table behind theirs. Stuart looked around in annoyance.

'Watch it. You're drippin' all over me,' he said, moving his stool out of the danger zone.

Helen laughed. 'You're really in a foul mood today,' she sniggered.
> playfully dodging
> the catcher
> coming through the rye

Stuart just scowled in return. He shook his head. 'No seriously, Helen, I want you to listen to me. Dont rush into anything with Douglas. You dont know him.'
> so oh

'And you do? Is that what you're saying? He's got some dark secret I dont know about?'

She had finished his portion too and felt much the better for it
> like I am fed

A Day at the Office

              u
              p
with the interference of this guy
     my brother
He offered her a cigarette. When she had lit it, he went on. 'It's not a matter of knowing him, I just think you should take your time. It's only a few months since you and Colin split up. What's the hurry?'

'No hurry. But can I ask you a question?'

'Sure.'

'Why ... ' she hesitated, 'should I take your advice? I mean, who are you? I hardly know you. You just come waltzing in, giving it the Hi-I'm-your-long-lost-brother routine and start giving me the benefit of your accumulated wisdom.'

He seemed to wince.

'I hardly know you, Stuart. And that doesnt mean I'm ungrateful for what you did when I was splitting up with Colin; that was different, I needed a place to go and I was glad of the space you made for me. But now that's all done with, and I'm doing fine now. I'm young, you're right, and I'm probably going to make some mistakes but that's my business now. Not Colin's, not yours, not even Douglas.'
                know what I mean
                  yourself
She watched him lean back on his stool, his eyebrows twitched and he rubbed his stubbly chin. He looked his age. More like her father than her brother
              fifteen years between them

'I'm going to get a coffee,' he said, and stood up. 'Do you want one?'

'Ok,' she said, indifferently. Inside she was mad
             oh crivvens
She could sense that Stuart wasnt at ease with himself. Even now after all the time he had wasted on drugs, he still couldnt do the simple thing that she had learned already
           just admit to failure
            self-confess it
             move on
She had made mistakes. Plenty of them. But nobody should have to live with guilt the way he did. She stubbed her cigarette as he came back with two cups.

As he passed her one, he said, almost in a whisper, 'Did you

know he was dealing?'
So that was it. She laughed. 'Of course. But he's giving it up once the gallery's open.'
Stuart shook his head slowly, gave a kind of pitying snigger that really annoyed her. 'You dont understand, do you? You havent got the faintest idea what's going on, have you? I'm not talking about antiques, I mean dope.' he lowered his voice. 'Coke.'

acola
nola
he
means
that
take a breath

ok now coolly

'I know what you're talking about. And I cant see how you've got any right, not after your escapades.'
He sighed and shook his head heavily. 'You dont understand. It was different then ... ' Helen interrupted, bored with it before he even started.
'I know, it was the swinging sixties, everybody was into it, it was ... what is it they always say on these phoney documentaries?

a more innocent time

You've told me before, Stuart. Remember? You're like an old soldier, hauling out your medals. What was that story about meeting Jimi Hendrix again? I think I've forgotten how it went'. She put her hand to her mouth and gave a huge, yawning sign.
Stuart said nothing. He sat looking down at his coffee cup. He looked miserable

really miserable

He seemed as if he was about to make some kind of dreadful confession,

abject
penitent
in the
pennytent

'If I was to say to you that I get this feeling sometimes with Douglas that he blames me for what happened to his brother, what would you say to that?'

> he cant be seer
> e us

'You cant be serious, that's what I'd say, I'd say you cant be serious.'

His eyes were like twin pictures of Saturn, greeny yellow and circled many times, he looked like Death
> too pathetic to be true
> still trying to put himself at the centre
> of everybody else's world

'I'd say that maybe it's your own guilt that's getting to you, that maybe you should sit down and think the whole thing through, then you'd see how stupid you were being. You cant be held responsible for what happened to him or anybody else.'

He leant forward, snapped, 'You dont know the half of it, lassie.'
> patronising bastard
> thinks I'm a dug

'Woof woof, Stuart.'

Stuart glared at her. 'Just dont get taken in, that's all. With all the rich kid bit, right?'
> stinger

'I dont know what you mean.'

'Oh no? Dont forget I went through it too.'
> your heeoo
> what's so special about
> poor dead heeoo

She stood up and put her coat on, then relented, bent down and spoke gently to him
> peering

'Look Stuart, I've got to get going. I only get forty-five minutes and I've got a couple of things to do. I cant stay long anyway. I'm sorry.'

He was the colour of a three-day old corpse. His eye sockets showed near as dark as if his skull had been bare
> burnt
> in the greater flame
> but he is no devil
> just an old guy to dodge

'You get off home to bed. I'll try to come out to see you on Sunday afternoon. We can talk about it then.'

He raised his head and gazed up at her. She was disturbed by how sad he seemed

      but it's the flu
He should never have come out.
  'Ok?'
  He sighed again, heavily, nodded. 'You dont understand, Helen. I wish I could tell you how I feel. I'm worried about you.'
       you you you
      he means helenme
        poor man
     it's totally genuinely pathetic
'Look Stuart, I do understand, really I do.' He was lost. Totally lost. She hesitated on the brink of leaving. She didnt really have to go just yet, and he did look ill. 'Will you be able to get home alright?'
  He stretched himself up, straightened out his curved spine and stood unsteadily at her side
        puttin it on
          the ritz
  'Yeah. I'm feeling fine. It's just so hot in here'.
  'Come on then, let's get you out of here. The wind will soon cool you off.'
  They went out of the restaurant and up the steps together. He seemed better, cheerier now. The weather wasnt. Great sheets of water swirling down from the buildings
       round the street corners
      terrible buffeting showers
She kissed him on the cheek and left him at the bus stop, standing in the shelter, and ran back to the casino, thinking
       I resent his interference
     I'm maintaining independence
      with limited resources
       I want involvement
        but on my terms
      I believe those promises
         Douglas
         I have to
       I've made mistakes
        plenty of them
     but no sense of guilt intrudes
      I acknowledge the fool
        that I was once
     that's more than Stuart can do
     in order to grow things must die
     admission of failure to thrive

A Day at the Office

acceptance of it as a natural conclusion
success squeezed between the mistakes
Stuart regretted his failures
the guilt remained untreated
a dormant infection
and his life was a ritual avoidance
tiptoeing so he wont wake it
while

She has been reborn.

1715
that busker in the doorway
makes a better living
and he has no one to demand it
round here
it's a cinch knot
on a purser's beard
real charity
**STILL WE HANG AROUND
THE OFFICE
IN PORT IN HOPE
OF WARMING THROATS AROUND
THE SINGLE BIGGEST FIRE**
yet
as night sets in
I'm standing on the fringe
of every reel
waiting for a walk-on part
a certain laugh
to take a taxi home
and not the crowded bus
like Ray
was really wasted as he wandered over the park from Blacklands, his whole body
seems to grow tiny
till there's nothin but my mind
and it is swelling
expandin like a balloon on a pump
wi every step
andinaminit
alhavwings
heading to the tennis courts, the hedges, sanctuary in the park.

There, sitting on a bench, he watched the players for a while, trying to use them as a point of focus to restore his concentration. His eyes were drawn to a couple playing singles. They were about his age but
far healthier
jees could I run still?
She was the better player of the two, running about the court returning his shots
she had the whites on
wee skirt knicks

with elegance but if the man got a chance to, he would rush into the net and thump the ball down at her feet. He was playing for his pride. Ray's interest was not in the tennis but in the game they were playing, in between the points too
      the guys turned on
like a mating dance of body poses, posturing and strutting, disputing
        ins and outs
        the doubts
       will she wont she
        can he?
It was so vivid to his doped mind that he felt like he was getting a rare insight into the human animal's behaviour. The signals she could send out were so powerful that players on adjoining courts were getting caught up with the two of them, and trying to outdo them. But their dances were not so strong
      so they are bit parts
        too
     like i ray on the sidelines
      the idlin audience
        wishing
       it may be
     not just the partner
        but
It was a while before he felt able to move away. He was thinking
     cant remember much about the Bible
      but there's that bit
      or is it even in there
    everything comes to he who waits
      if it's no it should be
      cos that's what it is
      everything did come
       does come
     if you just kept moving
     it was the fence sitting
the elaboration on the ball when all you had to do was stick it in the net
       like now
Suddenly he had the feeling that a lot of time had passed since he sat down there. Without a watch he couldnt tell for sure, but it seemed to be getting dark now and he would have to try to make a move. He could go and get a twenty-one back out to Eastercraigs or he could go up the Wayfarers and see if Gordon was about, he had the hash to sell

                    the hash
                    fuxache
                    where is it
                    jeez
                    not that one
                    no this pocket
                    k rist
                    i dontbelieve it
Hands rooting in every pocket, head trying to remember where he'd put the bit
                    that shawguy give me
his head disintegrates to panic
                    ohnow i couldnhav
i never left it in there did i?
                    ray you prat you fuckin silly prat
where is it man come on?
                    check again   again
                    again

                    oh no i don belive it

                    it's gone
                    i left it lyin in there

An awesome grim reality settled on him. The coup collapsed
                    the coo collapsed
                    no milk today
                    my love has gone away
Dejected, still disbelieving, he got up and began to retrace his steps hoping, against good sense, to just see the bit lying there in the grass. But it was getting seriously dark now and there
                    is no way back
                    on the same clear path
                    i trod here
                    no flashin sign
                    shazzambam
He was thinking now had the thing happened at all
                    was this guy real
                    or did i dream it?
                    worst thing was was it a wind up
                    that room the bedsit?
                    now there is no way to know
                    except goin back
The street lamps were on, in such a brilliant pattern that he

A Day at the Office

shivered. The rush of traffic through the cross junction was like a huge obstacle in his path. He hovered by the lights waiting on the green man, incapable of cutting his usual path through the driving lines of moving vehicles. Two or three guys came out of an off licence on the corner of the block and started heading up the street towards him. Something made him turn and stare at them though he knew that was the wrong thing to do. As they got nearer, the smallest of the three there fixed his eye on Ray who tried to look away and find a gap between the traffic. And then the lights changed
      glory me
     i'm paranoia free
and he was free, across the road, and out of reach.

When Ray went in, Freddie muttered a greeting and gestured to the tv.

–Incredible eh? Kids the most of them. He was watching gymnastics. Ray sat down at the counter on a high stool.

–World Championships isnt it?

Freddie nodded. –Aye. This is the last day. Individual events. Floor exercises.

For a while they both stared at the figure somersaulting over the screen. Then Freddie stood up.

–So what can I do you for?

–Cup of tea, Fred.

Freddie produced it without taking his eyes off the gymnast. Ray was hungry but had realised that he wouldnt have enough to buy a half of tobacco if he bought his roll now. Better wait to see if he could sell the grass. The smell of chips made it all the worse for him. He'd only had a packet of crisps, the egg roll and a Mars Bar since he'd left home in the morning, but what good was a smoke without some baccy to make a j with? So he sipped his tea and waited, enjoying the warmth and the easing of the pain from his blistered heel, and the toothache that was
     needling the frame

When the gymnastics ended, Freddie flicked over the channels and found some procelebrity golf.

–Anybody been in then? Ray asked.

–Saw your mate Gordon earlier.

–Oh aye? When was that?

–Bout two.

–Did he say where he was going?
–Back to work
himwork?

–Work?
Freddie stared at him
a mo

–Aye. He's got himsel a job. Did you no ken?
–Gordon?
–Aye. Said he might be in later though. The café owner reached for the button to change channels to a sports quiz. Freddie knew most of the answers. Ray waited. A few folk came in and ordered up mixed grills. Freddie shouted the details through the hatch to his mother.

Ray was managing to cool his racing brain. He was back in control and felt like it might be ok after all this Shaw
coodnaw
be wrong

He took his tea to a seat at the back, sat and smoked a roll-up and listened to the tv. He couldnt see the screen but that was ok, he had some heavy thinking to do
about
the nature of things
and where i stand
and do i want to move
i mean there's something here
this warmth
it's mine
a bit of it
is mine

But he was sick
really sick
about losing the swag
i can hardly believe it
i never do that
lose it like

And he started thinking about all that was out of reach, things that had passed through his hands and how once they'd passed out of reach, they were worth still more
the things that i've sold
and the peanuts i've got for them
in the buyers' market
where cash is the law

and the sickening sight of his guitar in the pawn, up for sale for seventy quid, when he'd got twenty-five for it. It was one of a

A Day at the Office

dozen or so that werent displayed but he could see them through the door to the back of the shop, where the fat woman chain smoked B&H. She reminded Ray of a book
                    a book i had
                    as a kid
                    twas
              Chess for Children
where the chess pieces had been depicted like cartoon characters and the queen was the archetypal henpeck, with a wee king half her size and
              the pawns were like me
              gettin burnt in the game
            of gold and grace and greed
she was just loaded, you could see it, she wanted you to see it. That was the art there, the display of wealth
              like this shawguy maybe
              no more than that
He kept the tickets still, tucked carefully inside the breast pocket of a jacket he'd bought out of the Oxfam a while before, but one he'd never worn. It was a perfect fit but somehow he was too small for it. He'd always thought that sooner or later he would make music, that he'd really learn to play the thing and write music too, but it was no longer
            the shining magic box to rub
            redeemable no more
        all a matter of adjustment never made
No distractions, that was what he wanted, just a place where he could settle down to concentrate his mind on something like that, no one listening through the wall shaking heads at his attempts before the thing was even born.

    It was the toothache. It was wearing away his sympathy. It was making him fevered. But where had all that time gone, where had all the things gone, that had passed through his hands and turned into gold on the chess queen's fingers?
              and what is i
              but useless tiny
              dont i know
      no satisfaction comes from pouring out
    But was it not the need that made the deal so perfect? And could there still not be some satisfaction in simply being, who he was or moving on, even though nobody knew him, or listened to the things he had to say? At school he had hidden in the sea of faces, pretending to having nothing to say, to avoid

being bullied by the others, the pupils and the teachers. He was made to go to remedial classes, but

i'm no dum
i learn to fake it
draw a circle round me

His silence was tolerated, and became a valid way of opting out. He learned the art of channelling adrenalin to make a great eruption out of angering, a temper fierce enough to frighten off the well-intentioned and the taunting types as one

so
no one knows me
no one knows
how far
i lean towards the outer rings

Outside in the playground, and around about the scheme, he had discovered the sweet secret of invisibility, a means of moving round the fringes without really being seen, so that he came to feel

i
have no right to enter
into anywhere
unless i know

that orbit is the only mode of motion

there

But this

shawguy
he wants me to move in
into
the inner
in-ness
an i can only do that
by opening up
the birdhouse
in my brain

–Hey, Ray. You watchin this? Some game, son, eh?

nodsmile
the circles plain

1745

after a day at the office
these numbers now mean nothing
to the night
on the bus i take my watch
and place it my pocket
now it is my eyes
that do the watching
from the top deck
as a man from down our street
drops his face on the pavement
while retrieving his hat
**HE MUST LEAVE
WHAT HE CANNOT CARRY
TOO MANY SUPERMARKET BAGS
OF UNENDURABLES
WEIGH HIM LIGHT
IN THE SCALE
THAT COUNTS**
we should learn to cast off
a regular losing
tune into la lune
Helenme she understands
the catharsis is underway
the gentle effusion
so routine and painful
the moonth full approaching
the devil's this pain
as she vexed herself over a young loser at one of her tables, who was moping over a cup of coffee
          a pleasant sad-faced boy
                 was he
who only stared up at her
                deserted
                by hope
when she laid the bill in front of him. But when she returned to the table, he had paid it and gone, even left her a tip. It was a case of
              intuitive failure
              care misdirected
   She should have been at home, soothing herself with herb tea and music.

The head waiter came over and told her that the duty manager wanted to see her. There was a phone call for her. It was ten to eleven and she had no idea who it could be

      hardly anybody knows
      I work here

She left the restaurant and walked along the darkened corridor to his office. There was

      uncertainty in my head

a shout as she knocked on the heavy wooden door.

'Come!'

She went in. The duty manager seemed uncomfortable, standing up as she entered, hanging above his chair

      like he was floating

She stopped just inside the door.

'You wanted to see me, Mr Groat?' The receiver was off the perch, lying on his desk top and he pointed to it as he spoke.

'There seems to have been some kind of accident,' he muttered, 'I couldnt really understand what he was saying. Sounded drunk to me.'

Frowning, he moved out from behind the desk and stepped around Helen to the door. 'Just take it in here.'

It was strange to be alone in this room where she had only been interviewed or reprimanded before. She looked around, delaying the moment when the disembodied voice would spread its bad news. When she finally managed to step forward and lift the receiver to speak, it was slow to answer.

'Helen? Is that you? It's me, Colin. Listen, Helen, I've got to see you. It's important.'

      orders and demands

She sighed. 'What's all this about an accident?'

'Oh I'm sorry about the story. It was just your boss, he said no phone calls for the staff, I had to make it sound important. I didnt mean to worry you or anything.'

He was talking quickly but Helen had stopped listening to him. She was angry, thinking how he had wound her up for nothing.

. 'Helen? You still there?'

Colin was not to be trusted. He was a liar.

'Helen?' She pictured his face at the other end of the phone and heard his insistent plea, as a sequence of bleeps cut through. Then his voice sounded again.

A Day at the Office

'Shit!'
The line went dead. She replaced the receiver, wondering if he would call back. If he did
>should I speak to him
>should I go to meet him?

The phone rang again. She hesitated
>hand and head disconnected
>stop hand dont lift it
>should I

before the impulse made her pick the receiver up.
'Helen?'
'What is it? How did you get this number?'
'Your mother gave it to me.'
>but why did she
>and why did she
>these interferences
>tolerate
>these people poking in

'Helen, I just want to see you. I've been thinking over everything you said. And I think you're right about a lot of things, you know.'
>what was this ploy
>these things
>this boyman ex mines
>hatching

'Helen? Are you there? I just want to talk to you for a while. These last few weeks, I've been thinking. I cant bear it without you. The house is so empty. I need you
>and each line
>is a song from the heart
>but
>his heart

'Helen?'
'I hear you Colin.'
>hear you speak
>of

'I just want to talk.'
>regression
>stagnation

'Will you meet me?'
>fragmentation
>the devil's aim

'Helen? I really love you.'
'I hear you.'

>speak my name
>from the safe house
>of nothingness

'Will you meet me? I'll drive down there and pick you up, we can go and have a meal and talk, that's all, just talk.'

'I'm working.'

'You dont want to work there do you?'

'It's ok. It's a job.'

>you're right though
>I dont want to work here
>but
>more than that
>I didnt want to be found here

'Whatever you want, Helen, I'll do it. Just give me the chance.'

She was wavering, his voice was the voice of someone she had loved, the boy who had taken

>my virginity
>my wholeness
>my integrity
>and in return he offered me
>what in his ignorance he thought
>was just what I always wanted

and now he was so close that she hated him for being

>the one still hanging on

She went to hang up. As she did so, he said something, she missed a bit of it, it sounded like

>win
>not you win again
>or I win
>just
>
>win

What he meant to say she didnt know but it was as if at that precise moment he signalled the end of the fighting to her. She knew that it was good right away, she saw his eyes had lost that flare

>theirflair
>but that card he sent a week ago
>was that really a poem
>him writing poems
>
>about me
>Hank Williams was it no

A Day at the Office

                 you win again
                 you lyin cheating
                 deceitin heart

The phone rang again but this time she did not answer it. The problem was

ring   we never really knew each other
ring   or we changed maybe too many times
                into things or images we imagined ourselves to be
ring   other than we were
ring   the mirror reversal taken for truth
                till now we are changed
ring   what we imagined really otherwise is now us
ring
                i could pick it up
ring   bye bye the way baby it's me
ring   i hear the music coming over the radio
                wait
                Helen wait
ring   I'll even clean the steam table
ring   Mr Groat
                just wait and hold that plate
ring
ring
                ring ringing in my head
                the ring I wore
                wore me out
                wore I worse
ring

Acting automatically, she felt herself leave the office and walk along the dimlit corridor towards reception. Everything was off-balance

                the whole day
                discordant
                warped

As she turned the corner into the reception area, she collided with Groat, and tramped on his toe with her heel, causing him to squeal with pain

                sharp
                but not stiletto stab

'I'm sorry,' she apologised. 'I didnt see you.' He glared at her, leaning against the counter rubbing his foot.

'Well, what's the situation?' Surprised at the directness of his question, she didnt know what to say.

'I'm not sure yet,' was the best she could do.

'But what's happened?'

>   more questions
>   poking in

She recoiled from his stare, looked to the floor and to the receptionist, who was watching from behind the desk with pained eyes, but grinning, savouring the disruption eagerly. It was too much to take, time to do something. The time had come to go. She stepped back, scratched her head, looked up and turned half around, then faced him. He leaned forward, like his head was a pin, trying to burst her

>   frankly mr shankly
>   this position I've held

She managed to mumble 'I've got to go,' stepped past him, away.

Groat came after her, towards the locker room.

'What do you mean?' he called, 'Where are you going?'

'The hospital.'

It wasnt really a lie

>   it is the kind of where

she needed to be going. He stopped looking in the fire door as she passed through it to the safe place.

'I'll have to deduct the time!'

The door swung shut

>   Win
>   he said
>   that's all he said
>   win
>   they say he smashed the windscreen when I left
>   in the morning as he went to work
>   he just lifted up a block from the pile that's to be the garage
>   I never wanted car anyway
>   well not when I read that 20%
>   of the world's carbon dioxide comes from car exhausts
>   but he's so narrow
>   all he thinks about is just his self
>   he cant imagine what it's like to be somebody else
>   just dropped it more or less through the windscreen
>   I'd have gone anywhere
>   it didnt have to be Egypt

ring
ring

>   it's just that I've always wanted to go there Colin
>   a kind of magnetism
>   ever since I was wee

ring   I mean a car would be alright but
ring   why dont we have a really romantic holiday

A Day at the Office

```
                        something to look back
ring                              on
ring                    when we are submerged
                              under kids
                no it is definitely not time to start a family
                  that's not the way I want to go about it
                              I want to
                                  to
                                 too
                                 two
                            two kids are fine
                           but so is none
                    so is one so is three so is four
                            I just want to
                                 wait
                  and I'd rather have a holiday than a car
                                  ok
                          if you really wantæ know
                                right
                    if we ever won the pools or anything
                               that is
                                 why
                                wait
                           it's the devil's work
        that thing when you're hovering on the edge of temptation
           conned into believing that the next thing's the right one
          that everything's just song and dance and pay the mortgage
                                  $
                           that old pop song
                      the somethings-man came by today
                     he said that he was giving them away
                         that I wouldnt have to pay
                                  $
                         and I couldnt say no $
                                  $
                        not to somethings like that
                          not to a price like that
                           not an offer like that
                           not today of all days
                          not a price like that
                              of all days
                              not payday
                                  $
                          la la la la la la $
                            lalalla lallala $
                           la la la la la la $
                         ayala ayallaway $
                                  $
```

The somethings-man came back today
he said I'd either have to pay
or he'd take them all away.
$
and I couldnt say no $
$
though it near nuff broke my heart
losing lovely things like that
lovely somethings like that
he couldnt let it go
not somethings like that
he said someone's
bound to know

$
la la la la la la $
lalalla lallala $
la la la la la la $
ayala ayallaway $

just
you
wait

>   *along lovers' loan*
>   *romance hangs the night*
>   *from the meat hook line*
>   THE INSECTS SWARM
>   OVER THE ARK
>   FILE OVER CORPSES
>   *as sweet papers tickle to rest*
>   *at the turnstile booth*
>   *by the side of the iron bridge*
>   *in the corner of the little man*
>   *with his soap box stand*
>
>   ah but we are safe so safe
>   from the voice of suffering
>   in the quiet of the suburb cell
>
>   THE WAR WONT BEGIN TONIGHT
>   though the tower may crumble
>   we'll eat our fill of life

though the dinner was no great affair. His mother was a very good cook but on this occasion there was nothing to prove, and no one to impress. Hilda Gilmour was an old friend. She had known Frances since school. Coincidentally, they had both been widowed in the same year. Barbara, Hilda's daughter, was the same age as Douglas. As children they had discovered the wonder of their anatomical differences among the bushes and trees in the gardens of their respective houses. As teenagers they had studied each other's changes from a distance, as models of the opposite sex, too close to be first loves

>   but
>   lovers
>   without enumeration
>   more essential than that
>   it's closer than close

And when their fathers died, his first in the summer, hers only a week before Christmas, it was as if they had shared the same bereavement

>   unfathered vapour
>   haunting us

She was the nearest thing to a sister he had, and he wanted to

like her. But she was so terribly sophisticated in her manners now, the wife of some
      highflying
      young
      allAmerican
executive, living in Miami. The last time they met, he found her hard to talk to. But there was so much death about, Hugh's funeral still strong in mind
      the great clam shut
      speechless
      perhaps this time
      be better
When they arrived, she was delighted to see him, and made a great fuss of greeting him. He accepted the superabundance of affection. Despite the face of carefully applied make-up, the girl was still there beneath, impish and exuberant. Frances and Hilda went into the kitchen, leaving them alone to drink their sherry on the sofa
      she
      sis
      miss
      ms
      mrs
   moments no more than changes making
      he
      his
      this
      place
 Barbara flicked her hair away from her eyes and sipped her drink. «So how're things, Dougie?» she asked.
 «I cant complain. What about Florida?»
 She peeped at him over her large red rimmed spectacles.
 «Florida's ok. Too hot for me sometimes.» She sighed. «Damn these glasses. I had to take my contacts out this morning after the flight over.»
 «And Desperate Dan?»
 Barbara pouted and frowned. «Dont call him that. You know his name's Danny.»
 «Well how is Danny then?»
 Her face became serious. She glanced at the opened door, through which the sound of their mothers talking filtered in. In a whisper, she said «We've split up,» then heaved a great sigh. She seemed to be on the point of crying

> or was she steaming
> if
> unfathered
> if vapour

He read the situation clearly was she actually
> broken
> hearted by this
> wounded knee
> the secret of americee
> the beautiful

«You havent told her yet?»

She checked the door again, then shook her head. Douglas didnt know what he should say. There she was staring at him, the little girl with the big secret, asking for his confidence, again. Asking for his time. He wanted to help her, he wanted to be able to care, to say the great wise thought that should be in his head but he couldnt find it there
> eloquence in mind
> holds up its hand to answer
> but I cant contact it

couldnt hear it. All he could do was lean over and squeeze her shoulder weakly. Somehow it seemed they were both too old for this game now
> yet always playing
> even when asleep

«And neither have you, it seems.»

«Sorry?»
> what's she

«Or do I read your situation wrongly?»

«What do you mean, Barbar?»
> pet name slip out

«Helen isnt it? Your little secret.»
> how did she
> had she
> in too close been?

«What are you talking about, Barbara?»

But there was no time for her to reply. The clatter of plates rang through from the kitchen, heralding the arrival of the trolley laden with dishes. Douglas stood up.

«I'll pour the wine,» he volunteered.

Barbara sniffed and drained her glass as he passed. There was a look in her eye he recognised, that twinkling mischievous look from their shared youth
> as if she'd really come home

Hilda and Frances fluttered round the table.

«It's so nice to have you all here tonight,» Frances beamed. «I cant remember when the house last felt so lived in.»

Douglas looked at her
                she means

She stopped for a moment, smiled wistfully at him. The sadness seemed to be spreading into nostalgic gloom, infecting them all
                but past
                  was it
                    still
                  not active
              through imagination
          real in the here and the done with

Barbara was silent, hiding behind her hair and her glasses, as Hilda distributed the plates, tucking wise wisps of long grey hair from her temples back as she leant over table, while Douglas poured the chianti. Frances served her meatballs in an Italian style sauce, a recipe cribbed from a cookbook many years before, since memorised and added to
            those little touches make the diff

Hilda sat down and tasted the sauce.

«You know Frances,» she said grinning, the German accent still clearly evidenced in her English though she'd lived in Scotland since before the war, «You could write a book on ninety-nine ways to cook mince.»

Douglas held back on his amusement. He knew the comment was intended as a compliment, but wondered if it would be taken as such
              or spit back

His mother simply laughed.

«I'm sure there must be one in existence already, dear.»

He let his chuckle out
              it's gamesplay

«So Barbara darling, tell me how you are?» said Frances.

Barbara flashed a glance at Douglas, then answered lightly «Fine, Frances. Although I really do not like the Florida climate. I mean, it's taken me a while to decide but, after a few years, I think I can honestly say it's really far too hot.»

This seemed to come as something of a shock to Hilda. She didnt say anything but shot a look at Barbara curiously
           as if perhaps its meaning to her

                              the metaphor semaphore
                                    leaving
«Oh. So do you think you may be moving somewhere else?»
                              that you again
                              her or they?
                                    merged
«It's possible,» she said and returned her mother's stare, bravely.

«But I dont want to think about that just now. I just want to be with my oldest friends and,» she looked again at her mother, «family.»

Hilda smiled, but the friends and family were few now, three men were buried,
                        husbands two and one sad son
and Douglas knew how she had felt that Barbara left her, when she married, in favour of Danny's mother
                         remember Ma saying
                                    but
The meal was proving an ordeal for Barbara. She laughed nervously. Frances smiled, leant forward, laid her fingertips on Barbara's forearm and said, with a glance to Douglas
                              she is
                         a little woman
                   shrunken now or am I bigger only
                    I'd like to see it how it was
«Well I must confess, I'm none too happy at Douglas' behaviour of late. He's been very secretive. I dont know if he's said anything to you dear but, well I've got my suspicions that he's got himself involved with some girl.»
                                    giel
Barbara seemed relieved that the focus of conversation had shifted from her
                              that look
«I wouldnt be surprised. I ran into an old friend today who was telling me that Dougie is quite a figure in the west end art scene now.»
                         Mother beams proud
«A gallery no less.»
                           that look means
«So I hear.»
                         playful pretty lies
«In fashionable Blacklands. And it is becoming so, though

who'd have ever thought it years ago?»

Hilda shook her head frantically.

«It was a place you simply didnt dare go when we were girls.»

Frances turned to Barbara once again. She made a show of whispering to her but the tone of voice was playfully too loud.

«And the girl. Did she mention the girl, this friend of yours you spoke to?»

embroideration

«Very pretty, I heard.»

go

«I see.»

between petty lies

«And her name?»

but no

Barbara looked at Douglas

dont show you're angry
relents

«Oh she didnt say.»

smoke
without fire

«And these friends in the west end, he's always shutting the shop during business hours, which is hardly a business-like approach.»

She was speaking ironically no doubt but

beware
going under the bridge go s-sip the wine

but
she knew Helen's name before
it couldnt be Stuart could it
but she said she

or was that ma

when I dropped him off
in town perhaps
Minnie?

Hilda swung a change of tack. She picked up the bottle by the neck, stood up and refilled everyone's glass. She winked at Douglas out of sight of the other two as she did so

or Joyce?
no
Stuart

A Day at the Office

            Barbara coming out of a shop
                I can hear her
         Hello there remember me?
               At the funeral
        we talked about dying
The game was over but the set went on.
«And Danny, how is he right now?»
«Oh missing me, I expect, having to do everything himself. Though he is remarkably good at taking care of himself. For a man, that is. In fact there are times I feel quite superfluous.»
              Hilda's frowning
The lightness of the talk seemed to irritate Barbara, though she was very good at playing along and didnt seem to mind scrutinising him in the way that she herself had resisted. Douglas could see how she was suffering
              she wants to say it
                  simply
                    cant
but try to make an effort at lightweight chitchat to get her mind away from their secrets.
«Did you see what they've done to the old station,» he mumbled, but she wouldnt talk.
«It's a desperate shame I think. All that modern tube steel stuff, it really spoils the integrity of the building.»
She just kept picking at her food like a
                mouse would
staring glumly at her plate. Sooner or later, either his mother or hers would notice and be sure to make some enquiry, and then who could say what would happen. It was potentially precisely the kind of emotional eruption he despised
           the sort of soapsinkdrama
                poperama
   melodramatics that they loved to watch on television
       or Puccini's punctured heroines
              Madama Butterfly
                one fine day
           my prince will return
                in chiffons
But thankfully Hilda and Frances were too caught up in their discussions of a planned charity fair and the moment passed uneventfully. The word that would release the flood building up behind Barbara's glasses was not spoken.

By the end of the main course, she had recovered something of her poise and it seemed as if she would survive the ordeal. Finding a suitable time to break
the story would of course come later
They sat for a while discussing the potential shape of Europe following the events of the previous season. From her animated expression, Douglas could see that Hilda had something to say about the reunification of Germany.

«You know I could not believe it when I was back in Germany at Christmas, how different people's expectations had become.»

No one leapt in to continue the conversation.

«It will be the final healing of the wounds of war,» she went on.

Douglas looked up. «Yes, but what are they going to do with all the troops.» He spoke partly in earnest, partly in jest. «They'll have to find them another wall to defend.»
move the conversation
far from Florida
His tone was too flippant for Hilda's liking, he could tell from the way she tossed her long grey hair back, and raised her chin as she stared at him.

«Douglas dear, there are other areas of the world in which their presence might be better deployed, for instance in blocking off that ass Qhadaffi.»

«So the new enemy is the Arabs?»

«No, not the Arabs generally, just those dictator types.»

«You mean the ones who insist on doing things their own way instead of simply toeing Washington's line?»

«The ones who do wrong to their own people.»

Her tone was one of great tolerance, as if he was a mere novice who knew nothing of the complexities of world politics
which may be so
but same true of you
Frances got up to fetch the fruit salad.

«I wish he was as interested in the welfare of his own poor country as he is in that of others,» she smiled
quite snidey
«You mean come and join your local branch of the Snip.»
keep it light
Barbara laughed and looked at Douglas quizzically. «The

A Day at the Office

snip?»
that's it now
we'll have you out in no time
Frances faked amusement. «It's his latest way of demeaning the good work done by the Scottish National Party. He seems to think it's funny.»

«Well it is, the idea of political castration.»

He looked at Barbara, who glanced at Frances and her mother. Their laughter varied by degrees
but it is
gunnygoof
ha he ho aye
ha he ho aye
aye aye
«Well I dont agree with their stand on the Poll-Tax myself,» said Hilda, «but yes, I can see the need for nationhood. I've said it many times. As long as it doesnt degenerate into anarchy.»

«Hear hear,» Frances called
quite mildly
poll-tax was an anomaly for her
and Sillars had her worried after Govan
she only trusts them when they're ineffectual
«It's not that I'm against some kind of devolution, I just happen to doubt the wisdom of having a party composed of such strange bedfellows,» Douglas said
which was true sentiment
a sediment of heart
«Sillars for instance.»
she shudders
«Sillars is not the party mass.»

«I didnt know there was one.»

«Ha ha aye aye aye»

Barbara seemed unable to contain her disenchantment any longer, putting her fruit salad aside almost as soon as she began to eat it.

Concerned, Frances looked up at her
a word may be enough
«I hope there's nothing wrong with you, dear?» Hilda interceded.

«It's just a question of the readjustment. I'm tired. Jet-lagged I think.»

«An ex-airhostess jet-lagged? Now there's a thing.»

Barbara smiled weakly at Douglas. «And I feel like I could do with a little air. It's very close in here.»
       too so for comfy

Douglas could see that his mother was a little winded by this criticism of her created atmosphere. But as soon as the dessert was eaten, and everyone had finished, he suggested that he and Barbara should take a walk down to the local pub. She readily agreed. Frances protested strongly.

«But wont you wait for coffee? Brandy?»
      mother is upturned
      capsized

«It's the walk I really want, Frances,» Barbara said brightly. «That and the chance to catch up on what's been going on.»

At this she took a hold of his arm, and leaned heavily on it.

«Yes, and I could do with a beer, Ma. It is hot in here.»

«Beer,» she said, as they left the dining room together, «What do you want with beer when I've a beautiful cognac here?»
      but youth walks out
      the tower falls

> in this part of town
> a door shuts on
> ME
> i prepare the ground
> put down some roots
> *at dawn for nightfall*
> *a new birth for the self-alone*
> the tuber sprouts a head
> the head opens its eye
> sees thinks
> it's not enough to simply grow
> i want to travel
> i want to walk
> the plant advances
> it wants to read the paper
> wants to watch teevee
> to engage the world
> talk over Saturday's games
> with the lads in the corner
> aspire to the stardom of here

and Ray's cup was long cold when the door of the café opened and in walked Gordon. He was wearing a long white apron and a frilly cap on top of his big bristly head. Ray and Freddie burst out laughing.

–What do you reckon then, boys? Neat eh?

Gordon grinned. He turned full round, arms outstretched.

Freddie shook his head and said half seriously, –Mad bastard!

Ray snorted and laughed, then frowned.

–You got to wear that gear all the time?

Gordon sat down on the stool next to him. –Naw. I only stuck it on to give yous a laugh. I borrowed it aff one o the lasses in the factory.

–Whit is it you're doing then?

–It's this pizza run I was tellin you about. Mind, the one my brother-in-law used to do? Och it's easy money, man. Aw you do is pick up a load of pizzas and take them round all the shops and cafés. Cash in hand.

He laughed and pulled the hat and apron off.

–So how many you wanting, Fred?

Freddie scowled at him. –I dont need to buy pizzas. My old

lady makes the best pizzas going.
 Gordon girned. –Sure, Fred. I'll take four hamburger rolls and a cup of coffee.
 Sensing the windup, Freddie laughed too.
 –Sure you're no wantin the wine list as well, bigspender?
 Ray's hopes of selling the grass had risen
cash in hand
Gordon had said. As Freddie turned away to get Gordon's order on the go, he caught Gordon's eye and thumbed towards the booths, as he got down from the stool. Gordon caught on and followed him over. When they were sat down, Ray pulled out the bag and passed it to him under the table.
 –Want to buy half?
 Gordon examined the stuff, then asked in a whisper –How much?
 –Eight.
 –Thirty-two a quarter for that? You been done.
 Ray sighed and smiled. –Best African bush, he shrugged.
 Gordon burst out laughing. He shouted over to Freddie. –Hey, Freddo. This bloke's a conman. You shouldnæ let him in here. He lowers the tone.
 Freddie glanced up. –Impossible, he called back.
 Ray relented. –Alright, seven then. I need the cash.
 Gordon smiled and agreed the bargain with a smarmy handshake.
 –Done, he said, –An that's you I'm talkin about.
 The deal settled, Ray's stomach began crying out for food again. He got up from the table, and went to order his egg roll and another cup of tea, then went into the toilet. In the cubicle, he took about half the grass out and placed it in his empty tobacco packet
transference
Then he flushed the pan out of habit and went back to the booth. Gordon was already tucking into the second of his rolls. Ray passed him the two bags of grass under the table and Gordon chose the bank bag, then passed him seven singles he had counted out in readiness. Ray's egg roll arrived and they ate in silence, then Ray ordered another and roused Freddie's temper.
 –Why cant you lot make up your minds?

–It's delayed action, Fred, Freddo, ken? Must be aw that monosodium powder you stick in the mix.

Freddie brought Ray's roll when it was ready, huffing a bit, but Ray could see he wasnt really uptight. He liked to pretend to Gordon that he was a tyrant, it was the only way he knew of checking him. Ray ate the roll quickly. He could see that Freddie wanted to get started closing up.

–Am I gonna have to throw yous out or what? he said, taking the empty cups and plates from the table. Gordon looked up and grinned.

–Got a room for the night, mine host? I cannæ face the walk efter your delicious fare.

–I thought you'd got yourself a motor?

–Naw, that was just for the pizza run. It's the brother-in-laws, he lets me take it afternoons.

They left the café aimlessly, exchanging a few friendly insults, and began wandering up the hill from the cross. The drizzle was falling steadily but it was light enough for walking to be on. Cars flashed past in a stream of lights
<blockquote>
another cosy world
that smell of vinyl
and the heater on
Dire Straits just a band
</blockquote>
–Wish it wis my fuckin motor, Gordon muttered.

They stopped in front of a hifi shop. The different systems were all set out in the window with price cards and post-Christmas reductions. Gordon pointed to a compact disc player.

–That's for me, man. Pure sound. I'm gonnæ save up the money I make on this pizza run and buy one.

Ray sniffed and shivered. The rain, though not too heavy, was getting through his coat, and the duffle bag was collecting it and running dribbles down his leg as he walked. CD systems were
<blockquote>out of reach</blockquote>
beyond him. He could pretend he didnt care but he did. Gordon was still rattling on as they walked but Ray wasnt listening. He had a smoke in his pocket and a few quid, but his heel was nipping again, the toothache was still working against peace, and he was tired of walking
<blockquote>chappin</blockquote>

> chappin

The shop front glam ended and gave way to a posh residential area

> the houses are all set back from the road
> at the end of driveways
> half hidden by trees
> no cars in the street
> all safe in the garage
> no sound escape
> the lives being lived here
> sealed behind their doubleglazing

The whole feel of the place was alien to him. He felt like chucking a stone through a window or letting off a banger, just to get some reaction, just to prove to himself that he was really there. But what was the point? What difference would it make? Another black mark against his name, another ticking off

> another downer

The rain was getting heavier and the bus shelter up ahead was too great a temptation. They ran on a bit to get under cover.

Inside, Ray leant back in the corner, and looked around at the near non-existent graffiti. Even the shelter was strange. He swung round and kicked the perspex hard with very little backswing

> the impact satisfies
> næ muckle

–I'm really seriously pissed off.

Gordon was subdued now. Ray saw him glance over, unsure what to say. He turned and pretended to peer into the distance, looking for a bus coming down the road. After a minute, he turned back quickly and grinned.

–Ach come on, man. We'll go an smoke this grass, listen to some sounds.

But Ray's mood had really soured

> to be back in this næ world
> goin back

–Fuck that, he said. –I'm fuckin sick an tired of listening an watching, an waiting for fuckin buses. I wantæ have some money in my pocket, ken.

Gordon looked away down the road again. He cleared his throat and gobbed into the water in the gutter where it ran

away through the grating. He started toe-ending the shelter, like he was keeping time to some rhythm in his head, then he glanced up.
 –You could try lookin for a job.
 –A job?
 –Aye, why no?
 –There's næ fuckin work. Where've you been for the last ten year?
 –There is so work. You got to get oot an look. You've never tried.
 Ray stood up and stared at Gordon. –I dont fuckin believe my ears. Whose side are you on, chap?
 Gordon looked away. –It's right though. You could get somethin. You got O levels.
 –Zero levels?
 –Naw, seriously. It's more than I've got.
 –Have them then. Better still, I'll sell them to you, now you got all this ready cash about.
 Ray scanned the distance for a bus. Finally a number 21 came crawling down the hill. They went upstairs and Gordon pulled out his straights. A kid sitting with a couple of his mates on the back seat with a ghetto blaster came over and tried to tap Gordon for a fag. Ray turned his head to look out at the wet
starless night above
but wan
wee wan
strugglin
The bus went slowly down the back of the hill and through the roundabout onto the ringroad, then swung right to the east between the two halfs of Eastercraigs Park. In the distance, he could see the five tower blocks standing on the city's margin
like they were made out of bricks of light
like they didnt consist of anything solid at all. Gordon was winding the wee kid up about smoking. That was the trouble with Gordie, he'd never grown up. He had a kid's sense of place and time
a likeable big galoot
the same wherever he went
great in certain circumstances
to have this big bloke around who could force himself on folk

in a friendly way, but there were other places when he should just keep his trap shut. Like when the old dear died. At the funeral, Gordon had cracked a joke and the old man flipped. But the thing was, Gordie didnt even know what it was he'd done wrong he was just so fuckin clumsy
stick him in the middle of a football park
he'd knock the posts down
if they went up the house an Erchie was in
no tellin what might happen
—So where are we headed then?

Grinning, Gordon let the boy take the fag he'd been offering him, then aimed a good humoured swipe at his ear, which the boy ducked. He turned to Ray.

—What about yours? he asked. —You ken whit my Maws like about swag.

Ray nodded. —Aye, so long as Erchie's out, then.

The bus reached the terminus beside the flats. Wet already from the walk up the town, they took their time and strolled down the steps onto the concrete semicircle that ran around the foot of the tower blocks. The lift was out
still broke
so they climbed the stairs.

There was no sound from inside. Ray opened the door with his key. Erchie was out right enough. But the place was freezing and he'd left a helluva mess of a fish supper over the settee. Ray tried the electric fire but it didnt come on. He went to put a fifty pence in the meter but it still didnt work. The bars were always burning out. So he went into the kitchenette and turned the oven full on with the door wide open, then rummaged about in the cupboards till he found a wee plastic tub of aspirins. It was empty. Gordon sat down on the black vinyl couch and started skinning up.

—Where'd you get this grass then?

—Jan's.

—She still livin wi that Joe?

—Aye.

Gordie grunted —Dont like that bloke.

—He's ok. Just hasnæ got a sense of humour.

Ray felt the blast of heat rising out of the oven. He shivered as he warmed on the back side only
but

A Day at the Office

                    the foot pain
                and the mouth pain
                  were easin up
          the foot and mouth dis ease
–Gonnæ put some sounds on?
–Aye ok.
                        oh i

Ray waited till he was properly warmed, then went through to his room. It was hellish damp, worse than the rest of the house. He raked about looking for his blaster, couldnt remember where he'd left it
                    bloody Erchie
–It's næ good Gordie. The machine's no here.
–It's in here, man, doon the side o the chair.
–Oh right.

Ray picked up a couple of tapes and walked back through. He pressed eject to open the player side and took one out
                    Erchie's tape
                    George Jones
              country an western crap
–That old cunt better no have broke this. He's always messin about wi this. I've warned him.

Ray opened one of the cassette boxes he'd brought and popped it into the player, pressed rewind.
–What's that you're puttin on?
–Wait an see.

The machine clicked, the first few chords rang out. Gordon raised his eyes towards the ceiling.
–Christ man not the fuckin Smiths again, is that all you ever play? You got nothin else?

Ray just grinned at him. –There is nothin else. You gonnæ pass that or what?

Gordon leaned over and handed Ray the smoke, a great big fat thing like he always rolled
                    full of tobacco
                death to the lungs
–Gonnæ play something else Ray?
Ray shook his head and sat down to smoke.
–Oh that's nice.

Whether Gordon was listening to the words or not was hard to say. It didnt matter. At least he was quiet for a while. Reverence was the byword for the Smiths. They were special

to Ray. But halfway through the side of the tape, Gordon sat up sniggering.
—This bloke at the factory, he told me this one. There's this bloke, right, out in the desert, miles fæ anywhere, right. He's got his dog with him, they're walkin miles through the sand, sun's blazin doon. The bloke runs out of grub, then water. Finally he cant go on. So he looks at the dug. It's you or me, Rover, he says, so he does the dug in, an eats it. For a bit he feels great, then after a wee bit, he's sittin there an he looks at the pile o bones lyin on the ground. Aye, he says, shakin his head, Rover would have loved them.
He burst into a fit of laughter as he delivered the punchline.
—Good eh? I thought it was a cracker when I heard it.
Ray laughed. But more at Gordon than the joke

the big galoot
head filled up wi daft jokes and stories
no room for anything else
no time to listen
he couldnt change if he wanted to
he'd never change
if he tried
he'd just get lost inside himself
disappear up his own arse

—Put somethin else on eh?, he asked again. —This is borin'.
—No.
There was something going on here, something was being measured, the space between him and Gordon maybe. The Smiths were the ruler he was using and if he was gonnæ get the truth he'd have to see it through

to see exactly who it was
was doing the eating
an who was getting eaten up
up down
straight stoned
some things like Gordie
stay the same

—I've decided I'm gonnæ get a place up toon, Ray said.
Gordon stared at him, surprised. —I heard that before.
—No outa my mouth.
Gordon snorted doubtfully. —Just like that, you're gonnæ get a place? Some dump of a room wi six other guys?
—No, just a nice wee flat, no sharin.
—Just like that æ? You're gonnæ get a place up the toon?

A Day at the Office

−Why no?
−Money man, that's the why no. Where are you gonnæ get that kinda cash? I mean you're gonnæ need a month's rent upfront an probably the same again as a deposit, that's if they'll let a flat tæ somebody on the dole. I ken the whole story, Ray, næ DHSS

yeah?
smartass you dinnæ ken the half
of the half of the half
ha ha
the lost eighth
the shawguy
oh i

Ray stared hard at him, Gordie, his friend. Gordon looked away
letsee
with a smile, Ray said −Well how about it? Lend us the deposit and I'll get it back off the Housing. They're payin rent for me at Jan's the now.

Gordon wouldnt look at him. −It's no that easy to get a decent place, Ray, he muttered. −Anyway I've no got that kindæ money.

Ray scoffed at this. −Come on Gordie, youve always got money. What about this pizza run thing you were tellin me about? Cash in hand you said, thirty quid a day wasnt it?

deduct half
for exaggeration

Gordon went pink. −Aye well, I wasnæ exactly tellin the truth there Ray.

−So it's only twenty? Listen, it would be like your place too, man, you could crash there whenever you wanted.

−No it's no that Ray. See it's full-time, above board. Ninety quid a week after tax.

For a moment Ray was stunned

stunneds
no the word

−You mean it's a job, a real Job Centre job?
Sheepishly Gordon nodded.
−Aye I'm off the dole. Just got fed up wi it ken?
Ray took the j

from his old mate
who had changed after all

shocked into silence.

—But it's no just the money Ray, I mean you're gonnæ find it a lot harder than you think to get somewhere decent, man. When you tell folk where you're coming from, they just tell you to fuck off. Posh folk, ken? I'm no bullshittin, man, I ken loads of folk that have given up tryin.

Ray snorted, annoyed. He wanted to believe this Shaw was different
that i
ray
am different
—That is so shite. You dont have to tell anybody anything.

Gordon tried to soothe him. —Well maybe it is different for you. Maybe you could get away wi it. You always were a bit different
meaning
—You can put on the posh voice a bit. Probably your maw's influence. Her being from up north and that. An anyway, this places alright. You ken where you stand here, man. I'm happy here
a pig in shite
—I'm gettin out, Ray answered sharply. —An I'll tell you somethin. I've got a place sorted already. I dont need the money. I just wanted to see if you'd do it
did i overdo it
The big bristly head lifted and dropped
understanding?
the space that was being measured gapes open
now no words can fill the gap
just float i
with the music
silence

.

for a whole track
The tape clicked off. Gordon picked up the bag with the grass in it.

—I'd better get movin, he said
me too
—Think I'll keep a hold of this for the morn efter work
ray
ray
you stung him man
—I gottæ be oer at the factory for half seven, he said, twisting

the top of the bank bag over, sticking it in his pocket.

He looked at his watch as he struggled to get out of the sunken settee. Ray tried to offer him a hand but Gordon ignored him.

–Pheugh, he breathed. –That stuff's lethal.

Ray said –I'll walk down to the chipper. I fancy a supper or something.

They went towards the door, then Ray caught sight of Gordon's carrier bag, with the apron and cap inside, lying on the floor in the corner
     the jester's bag
–Here, he said, –better no forget the uniform, but Gordon didnt laugh, just took the bag as they went out onto the stairhead. The big fella seemed to lose his balance or something, he went skating down the first flight of steps, and got up rubbing his head. He picked up the carrier bag.

–I was just away tæ say I was ready tæ crash oot, he grinned.

Ray smiled, glad to see the humour wasnt dented.

–You'll need to look after yoursel. We cant have you goin on the sick already.

They clattered down the stairs and out into the night. The rain had stopped at last and the moon had appeared. It was floating up above the top of the block to the south, partly hidden by a thin gauze of mist. It seemed to Ray
      like an intruder
    a peeping tom with a flashlight
   at the window of a fast moving carriage

choosing to befree time
take plenty of liquid
run in the bath
BUT NAKED AFLOAT THERE
I SEE THEM PEEP
ON TIPTOE
AT MY WINDOW
I DONT MIND
IT'S PART OF THE JOB
TO PUT UP WITH THE COMPANY
sit down with hot news dinner
microwoven à la carte delight
tonight
like the ad people eat
count calories in captions
watch the screen version
of the food before
chewing over
the events of
a day at the office
a plane has crashed
a politician lied
an actor wrote a book
WHAT ELSE IS NEWS
the headtalkings tie

but
she is not new
this city
she is not ours
she is the coral reef
we explore till we give up
our bones
nothing is ever made new
make it together
nihil nix
zeroing out at the end
cramped in the upstairs room
the mattress behind the door
that face at the mirror

>   *again again*
>   **but with Helenme**
>   **her head on the moon**
alone inside, in the staff locker room, it was different. She sat crouched down on a chair, till her head was clear and there was nothing more to think about, nothing to solve
>   no puzzle
>   just get out
>   go
She stood up and pulled off the offensive skirt and blouse, opened her metal locker and stuffed the clothes onto the shelf at the top. She didnt care anymore. She was walking
>   out
>   it was a dud job
>   they could keep it
Once she had her own clothes on again, she felt better
>   calm
>   whole
The locker was full of things that had accumulated over the months. She pulled some out with the intention of sorting through them. But most of it was rubbish. And all of it was tainted by being here. So she just dumped it, the uniform too, into the plastic swing-bin by the sink.

She took her bag and went out the door. Groat was standing at reception ready to intercept her. She didnt look at him, but headed straight for the revolving door out onto the street.

'Helen?' She didnt answer.

'You'll be in tomorrow?' His tone was a demand.
>   tomorrow?
The idea of a tomorrow lightened her mood. It was natural that there would be a tomorrow and that it would be meaningful after this. She felt an impulse to tell him that, to fetch the frilly blouse out of the bin and stuff it down his throat
>   make him eat it
but she carried on, skipped down the three steps to the door. A middle-aged couple in evening dress were coming out of the restaurant, making ready to leave. She barged past them, past the doorman, through the revolving door, into the night.

Behind the smoked glass front, she saw the duty manager mouth dumb apology to his precious clientele
>   oh it was sweet to be free

The clock above the jewellers she had read before to see if she was late for work could stop now
<pre>
                    at five to
                    midnight
                   ball eternal
              a star had risen and fallen
        to be caught by the hands of the goddess night
               while the moon is on the rise
</pre>
A taxi passed with its *For Hire* up but she wanted to walk. To feel secure in herself, out on the street. In her city
<pre>
                because it is my city
                  to go anywhere in
                   to do anything in
                    to be anyone in
         but never to forget what made the me as I is
</pre>
At first smiling, then laughing, she was walking down towards the river to the heart of all the life there. Her footsteps were springs which sent her skipping and tripping, yet somehow kept her moving freely for the first time in years
<pre>
                  to do what I want
</pre>
She stopped high above the rippling water, by the stone embankment, looking down onto the lamplit moonlit sparkle and up from there across the plug of rock on which the castle stood, to the castle that then seemed to settle itself upon the craggy seat. Its walls were a pattern of light and shade, shiny in the dampness, as if the entire structure had been bathed in lacquer. It was an
<pre>
                    old god icon
         worshipped in the light of electric city
                    omnipresent
               the symbol of that city
         on a huge catalogue of tacky souvenirs
                    printed on
                     packets
                        of
                      short
                      bread
</pre>
She walked. Along the riverbank, trying to listen to the river slipping quietly under the bridge but disturbed by the grind of car engines, by the odd knots of people wandering about, partygoers, disco club kids, drunks dithering over dregs
<pre>
            where there was nobody at all
             it was easy just to slip into it
                    think nothing
</pre>

A Day at the Office

                    note it
                    notice
                    zero out
                    go under
                    the bridge
                    with the water
                    i want to
                    rain with the rain
                    just that
               but here there is a centre
               a lost god of property
               powerless now
             except as token root in time
          for tourists hungry for a snap of history
              yet once the seat of royalty
            where kingly queenly lugs were bent
             by the tricky tongues of underlings
           that schemed and fought to reach and get
         where decisions of importance might be made
             now a museum in a city full of them
              the stronghold of the occupying army
              which is paradoxically our army
                why not turn it into a casino?

She walked. The castle seemed to swell and grow as she approached it, till it was like a body in the heavens grown to be a dying star. It was the
                    war man's chariot run wild
    The statues of the famous men along the river walk
                      seem to turn
             pointing down from their pedestals
         like they are saying, just who do you think you are girl
                dismissing centuries of tradition?
              what right had she to turn and walk away
              when they were frozen by their histories
                  their time allotment gone
                  now trapped inside biography?

                    to rebel was to what
                    act up
                    think wrong
                 move away from what was done
           not to have your feet stuck in cement bases
                    to reform

              like the castle polished and maintained
                they had no power these men
              unless your mind allowed their minds

to enter into yours
this penetration is a form of fucking
and often fucking up
though they could point the way
she could move and walk it
down the line still
they could influence
she could choose
to

step

onto the suspension bridge, along the walkway. Lights fluid
on the water, the castle and its guard of stonemen passing now
behind her to the east. Lights fluid on the water
moonshine bright tonight
easing to forgetting
go words
smell of the water and fuel oil mixed
filth on its way to the open sea
the estuary the sea the ocean
there is only one ocean
our names are for different bits of it
wait no more
for the shipyards now are quiet
and the cranes have gently fallen
let's have a wild mountain time
you and me
in these wonderful
water sports facilities for the leisured classes

the shipyards are so silent now
statues themselves
vainglories now redundant at the city's heart
useless running words languid river never coming back
understanding nothing but the syllable you're speaking
and no way you can turn the tap off
renewing something though
some need
maybe unfolding like time
what right was its to leave
was something made or was it patternless
just tangled net around the thinking part?

like faither
proud of his city
his castle

A Day at the Office

                    his river
                    his ships
            though his pride was the same force
                 as kept us
               at the foot of the hill
                  motor words
                   remember
                 packing in the car
            kids going to the place where
              the new house would be
           when the transfer came through

                something small and loose
    thinking about how the time when the letter came never came
                     to that address
                       the name
         the reputation of the scheme enough to trigger
              set to flick the switch of prejudice
         where tradition so much formed a part of how they thought
                    it was their fate
                and her fate here in this city
            no one outside knew how much it cost

   But what did all this mean to the moon? Was it not all just delusion from there? To even imagine it as having importance is to give it importance, so how could she stand back and say, be objective
                there is only this me voice and how it now feels
                       to be so envisioned by you
                       is easy as being is for you
                    the dreamings become so for me

Yet the tradition which this castle symbolised
                    this castle with its rock
            was the single unifying factor for the people
                 who were variant in so many other ways
                         as rich and poor
                         as prod and pape
              yet that tradition repressed as it so unified
            calcifying bone of old instead of nourishing new
                      the new had to be
                         has sense
                    to be sense of too many
      the statues and the plaques commemorating past achievements
    inhibiting the natural desire to outreach the past through new achieve-
                              ment
        allowing the edges to wither while the stone stem thrives

                    organism of city
                    Jerusalem fallen
            your flesh is now bungalow land
                mini castles for houses
    patterns unbroken remain by the gaudy shop fronting
            commerce is visited by car
                    people check
                  coupons and rates
                shop wisely at Christmas
                 juggle figures to stay
                on the ladder rung world
              where no rung's insurance
            from a foot in the face from above

                that wee hoose we had then
                where Linmill I lived then
                 the name how I loved it
                and what a fantasia it was
                         at first
    to be woman of house with the gadgets all new
            and the chance to pretend to be old
                         in my
                         novice
                        maturity
                         home
            a place to be safe from the world in
A bottle bobbing in the murky water catches her attention.
It is for a moment her then she was it
                        and I is it
                       thus bobblin
                 and the waning moon
simultaneously and the river became the blacked out depths of
space
        ah river you fool me again and again with your movements
            I feel me attuned to your rhythms
                and sing with your song
              an Aeolian harp in the stream
              then lose it as you turn again

    Not having money nor the inclination to take a taxi, she
walks across the bridge and up the gentle slope on the other
side, through the deep ravine that was not a place for woman
to walk at night, the Coogait, emerging near the cross at
Blacklands.
            what was it Douglas had said about

> his grandfather riding around the cross here
> in his carriage pulled by two white stallions

And he it was who planted the only tree in the whole length of Atholl Street, Helen.

Passing the close where Mrs King's flat was she shuddered, no longer sure about how she felt. She did care, that was the terrible thing. She cared not only about the poor old woman, but about her mother and her father, and her brother and Colin and Douglas. But now she cared most of all for

> Helenme
> iI
> so put self side inmost
> go to see the old lady
> mental note tomorrow
> if strong toself then outgive hope
> to poor infirm and none too loved ones
> okdoke

There was inevitability alright about things happening but the nature of

> things could be not divined by the uninitiate
> and more than half of life is this
> this strange irrationale
> this twitchycraft
> of meeting and affecting changes in each other's lives
> no point questioning it
> in taking halfopenings and sifting through till the metaphor is found
> means to make
> the metaphor real too and if the symbol is displaced
> from symbolising
> the spell cant really work
>
> Caution!
>
> The motifs once in a person's mind remain there
> connecting in to all peculiar sorts of tangent meaning
> to be blind to these is to as Kundera I read said
> deprive oneself of a dimension of beooty
> and what else is there if not this beooty
> sweet colleen it is
> so true
> the vision of my human kind as clever animals

haunted her. Helen was thinking of invented deities to provide a means of understanding existence, of parasitic burrowings of humankind in nothing but the crust of the crust of the crust of the skin and turning to Baird Street

                    footsteps slapping weary now
she saw a skip full of rubble and bricks from a reno job. Her
eye was fixed on a brick standing up on its longside, on which
was stamped the name of the brickyard. Lennox. It was as if it
had been put there
                            for me
                            to find
                     by the hand of a fellow
                      a worker here maybe
                   whose symbol this brick is
                            the builder
She picked the brick up. It had obviously been used, there
was mortar stuck to one edge, but the letters L E N N O X
were as perfectly moulded as the day the brick was made. It
was surprisingly light, just the shape of the hand
                           my god
                       I never thought
             but of course the world is made to fit us
                          even there
It was a transmission of understanding such as she had
never known before in her entire life. Her soul
                      yes only my soul
responded   to the joy of being she
                        from Lennox
                       and it was such
              that it precluded thought of science
              of men as other than a boyish need
               to defuse fear of unknown forces
                      far more powerful
                   by mastering environment
                    but there is other way
              freeing of whole self from these fears
               acceptance of the urge for beaooty
                       only valid meaning
                          aesthetes all
                but what of the real and the way
            to full exposure to the world and interaction
                interference is the word I fear today

Her body was recharging itself for another moonth. The
moon was feeding her the depth of space. Helen turned from
thinking to her doorstep, took the key out as she climbed the
streetsteps and felt her aches relent.

these soap operas
are mediately functional
between
the incommunicable fact
of who am I
and the formless fiction
of the social we

PUT YOURSELF IN MY POSITION

without them
life would be limited
to what really happened

PASS ME THE DISHTOWEL DARLING
the dinner party's done with
and

the rain had stopped. The damp night air carried the odour of winter. But it was mild. What remained of the rhododendrons shone
like stiff tongues of plastic
in the yellow lamp light. Douglas stood a moment, watching the nothing as it didnt happen in the cul-de-sac, waiting for Barbara while she fetched her coat and touched her make-up
up
I am
aware of her panic only vaguely. When she appeared, he began to walk down the drive, a few paces ahead of her. Once they turned the corner onto the pavement, he waited till she caught him up.

«God! That was awful!» she exploded. «I felt so ... so ... »
awful
«I'm so glad you kept them talking, Dougie, thanks.»
«The least I could do.»
for myself
Douglas began walking again. He knew that she wanted him to stop so she could unleash the torrent, but he wanted to get to the pub where her pride would restrain her from the full emotional performance.

«I thought you did very well,» he said over his shoulder. «For a minute, I really thought you were going to blurt the whole thing out over the meatballs.»

She skipped forward a couple of steps.

«I wish you'd slow down, Douglas. I'm almost running, you know.»

«Sorry.» For a few strides he eased his pace. But as soon as he did so, she started talking about it again.

«I know I should have told Mother right away. All the way over on the plane I was rehearsing what I'd say. But when I saw her, standing waiting for me in the airport lounge, she just seemed so happy to see me, you know, I couldnt do it.»

He was lengthening his stride again.

«Not far now,» he muttered.

Barbara suddenly stopped walking and stood there in the middle of the pavement, her hands on her hips.

«You're really not listening, are you?»

He turned round. «Of course I am. But hurry up. We can talk about it in the pub.»

She hesitated, staring at him sadly, then curled her mouth into an appealing grin

cat ches hire
self

«Douglas ... ,» she pleaded, «don't be so ... so cold with me. Just wait for me a moment, please. Talk to me.»

But all he heard was

me me me

She stepped forward and grabbed his arm.

«I'm alright, really. Actually I'm glad, you know, that it's finally happened. I won't embarrass you or anything, promise.»

He submitted to her affections. They walked together down the tree-lined avenue, till it opened out onto the main road south, then along Baird Street to the door of Porter's Bar

celeb in num. wrks. of lit.
Rob. Burns drank imp. wenched here
mens club room
closet

Pushing the door of the pub open, the familiar red patterned wallpaper and carpet invited them in as if it were a warm womb they were entering. Porter's was a place they both knew well, though it was some time since either of them had been in. It had been his local when he lived with his mother, before he moved into the flat. And Barbara had spent time there, before she began her travels with the airline. She went to a corner table, sat under a glowing red lamp, while he went to buy the drinks.

«I've decided,» Barbara said as he put the glasses down on the table top, «not to burden you.»

«Oh? I thought you wanted to talk,» he answered, sitting down on a stool. She sipped her brandy.

«Yes, well I did at first. But I realise now that what's happened between Danny and me, it's not actually your concern, is it?»

«Want to shoot some pool then?» he said
        joking

She peeped at him over her spectacles
      different without contacts
       with those glasses
         attractive
          yes

«Come and sit,» she said, patting the seat next to hers.

He couldnt decide if this was one of her ploys. Or was she sincere in these warm gestures?
       letssee
      move over

«I mean I know you, Douglas. You never were one for sympathising. I suppose you take that from your father.»

He took a sip of lager, watching her.

«Anyway, let's talk about something else. What about you, Dougie?»

«Me?» He lit a cigarette, a little puzzled. «What about me?»

She shrugged. «Oh I dont know. Whatever you're doing these days. Remember I've been away quite a long time. Everything's changed.»
     nothing ever remains the same
       but
  the fire is constant though the flame burns out

«I dont know where to begin,» he said, then: «Sorry I didnt offer you one.»

She deftly avoided the temptation of looking at the cigarette packet. Douglas laughed
       at face of her
       avoidance

«Given up?» he asked and she nodded.
«So what else is new?»
«Ah-ah,» she wagged a forefinger at him. «You first, remember?»
He shrugged as he took a drink of lager
> liquor of corn
> sun's child
> of swoon in love in winter's depth

«Well you're obviously not living at home any longer,» she prompted.
He inhaled deeply, then blew the smoke in two mingling jets out through his nostrils as he shook his head.
«I moved out a couple of years ago. Do you remember the old shop over in Blacklands? In Foundry Lane?»
«Which shop?»
«My grandfather's shop,» he answered, then added with a hint of sarcasm, «the place where the family fortune was first multiplied.»
She thought for a moment.
«Was that the place we went once with your father, when we were little? It was all boarded up?»
«That's right!»
There was something gratifying in the fact that she still remembered, that they still shared memories
> of
> some simpler them
> than these
> no longer children we are

«You kept on at him afterwards to take us back.» Barbara gave a short nervous laugh.
«Did I?»
«Yes. Dont you remember?»
> must be buried
> that time we were touching

She shook her head. «And that's where you're living now?»
«Not in the shop itself. My grandfather left Hugh the whole block. I inherited it on my twenty-fifth birthday. The only condition was that we didnt sell it.»
She seemed
> really interested

«Sentimental old fool for a Victorian developer, wasnt he? So I had the place renovated four years ago. I live in the ground

floor flat and I let out the flats above. The shop's going to be a small gallery. Well it almost is now, in fact.»
Barbara smiled and sipped from her glass. «A gallery? In Blacklands? That seems a little incongruous, if you dont mind me saying so.»
         she's playing
         she knows this
        she told ma at dinner
       but go on explain it yourself
        see where it takes her
Douglas laughed. «Like you said, everything's changed. You'd hardly recognise it now from what it was like a few years ago. Lots of the old tenements have been sandblasted, there are trendy new shops and restaurants opening all over the place.»
«So you're a property speculator now, Dougie. I'd never have believed you had it in you. The last time I saw you, I really thought you were going to spend the rest of your life in that house with your mother.»
         what's this
         she's tease
«I mean, I understand what it must have done to you both, when Hugh killed himself, I really do, but I honestly believed you were there for life. I'm pleased for you, Dougie, sincerely. And it must have taken some strength on your part to do it.»
        flattery at work
She was leaning forward listening to him, her chin supported by clasped hands. He noticed that there was mock admiration in her face and it annoyed him. She didnt really care what he was doing
        it's just another tactic
        what she's doing now
      is just a way of getting back at me
        for what I earlier did
       to her first emotional appeal
      now she's using shared past
    to drive back me again into the dulled world
        I inhabited before
He felt his expression change visibly
       know that she saw it happen
«I suppose some of us are slower at leaving home than others,» he said quietly, staring into his lager. Then looking up, he added, «but some of us stay away once we've gone.»

>   the words were a small stinging hurt
>   which when launched made her flinch
>   and now am I sorry

He saw her sophisticated front slip away as her head tilted at an angle from him, just as if he had slapped her face.

«You're right,» she sighed. «The psychological umbilical keeps pulling us back.»

Of course, he knew, this was his cue, to probe into the depths behind that statement. He should have begun by extracting the hurt he had inflicted, then progressed to a gentle probing of her marital difficulties

>   the scripted role
>   no want to know
>   not ache the part

He had moved away from all that. He had found another more exciting game to play

>   the dealing
>   but here the bar is open
>   I am drunk and she is giving me
>   the full story after all

It was her version of the events which had led up to her running home from Miami

>   suburban adultery
>   American style
>   it is about as dull and petty
>   as expected it would be
>   and the only barricade against it possible here is drinking

She didnt seem to want anything from him after all, no advice or sympathy as he had feared. Unburdening required only his silent presence, the occasional nod or grunt. Had he been sober, this state of idleness would have irked. But drunk, it was all a soap opera, happening on another dimension from his, demanding only that he should tolerate its right to exist. He just watched her mouth opening and closing, her facial expressions as they

>   twist and relax
>   changing
>   modifying words
>   while she conducts
>   a one-sided dialogue
>   on the narrow issues that dominate her life
>
>   and yet
>   not listening

>   just watching
>   she's sweet
>   quite stunning
>   sexy
>   not a girl
>   a woman with past

He bought another round of drinks. As he returned to the table, she sighed, and went quiet.

«I'm sorry, Dougie,» she said at last, as the call for drinking up went out, «I really didnt mean to go on so. It's after midnight.»

He smiled at her drunkenly
>   but still

«It's ok, really, Barbar. I've really enjoyed getting pissed with you, you know that? Struth.»
>   she's sis always
>   the wee girl still inside
>   lovely

She flicked her hair away from her eyes and in doing so, knocked her specs askew, then giggled, at ease at last.

«I'm a bit tipsy. I think you'll have to carry me home.»

«Drink up then,» he said, trying to focus on his watch, «I'll give you a piggy back.»
>   if can muster savoir
>   not slip
>   crash hoot

The warm red pub was much less the womb, now that the bar lights were off and the street door was pegged open. They made their way outside. The night air was heavy and quite cold but the rain had stopped.

She took his arm and they lurched around the corner, back up the hill towards the house. They hadnt gone far when Barbara hauled him to a halt. She grinned mischievously
>   perked up now

«I've got an idea,» she said, slurring her words, «Why dont we take a taxi?»

Douglas frowned. «It's only a couple of hundred yards.»

«No ... oh ... oh!», she laughed, wagging a finger at him «You dont understand. Dont interrupt me. I dont mean to your mother's. I mean to your shop in sunny Blacklands.»

«Now?» he asked, wondering what she was up to. He gestured up the road.

«What about them?»

She leaned close to him and gripped his arm tightly. «Oh not tonight, I couldnt face them tonight. Not in this state.»

Lifting her chin, she whispered in his ear. «Dont you want to?»

> it would be like
> incest of secret collusion
> back in the bushes together
> if that how I read it is

«It might be fun.»

He looked at her, then down at the pavement, then up the hill towards his mother's house

> where the mothers plural await us

«Well, what do you say, do we go shopping or not?»

He smiled, he was just about to agree when suddenly she stepped away from him, letting go of his arm, and punched him hard on his shoulder.

«You thought I was serious, didnt you?»

> werent you

«Oh Dougie!»

> what is this game
> your playin not plain

«You didnt really think I'd do that, did you?»

> all bitched up
> with bitterness that girl

He carried on walking, mad

> walk on walk on

at himself for having been duped.

«Do-ogie! Dont take it like that. I just wanted to see if you had really changed or not. It was only a bit of fun.»

«Well you havent changed, that's for sure,» he said loudly, without stopping. It was just the way it had been when they were kids

> her teasing me falling for her tricks
> her stupid games
> or maybe it is me who is stupid

He could hear her giggling, a few paces behind, as they went up the hill. She called to him gently.

«I'm sorry, Dougie, honestly. It's just that you always seem to bring out the brat in me. I'm sorry.» She was returning to the voice of the sophisticate

> coaxing

A Day at the Office

He just wanted plain company. People who would say what they meant, without all these
petty
intrigues. He was no good at the games
never have been seen to be
but
Barbara had achieved mastery at a very early age. Maybe she was right. Maybe he had inherited his fathers
awkward unsympathetic naïve
way. As they neared the house, she caught up with him. His annoyance had subsided. She caught hold of his arm again. He wouldnt look at her, but marched her up the drive and the front steps.

«Honestly, I'm sorry, Dougie,» she said as they entered the hall. «I never could resist teasing you.» He slipped off his coat and hung it on the stand, then sniffed and giggled
pointlessly
all this
«No, you never could, could you?» he muttered.

He hesitated entering the lounge.

His mother took a long time to forget small incidents, like them walking out like that on her dinner party, and the last thing he wanted was to stir it up with her again, by going dashing in from the pub in a bad temper.

He went out through the back door in the kitchen, into the garden, before facing the noise in the lounge. Wet leaves from a maple brushed his cheek
that tree so weel kent
to the wee boy in me
this is the ageing rings that grow

it is january
pickin on me
again

o the smell of wet earth in the winter
is the song of Mahler's erde
and lovingly I tread on plants that live

calm self
return
incant the love of Mozart
rise transcend above the old self
that still lives here in this house

                    small spliff
                secretly in the dark
              how sweet the forbidden
            the best is always under cover
              unknown to mother father
                    brother all
          and only mine this space inside me
              which is cosmos in itself
                  relating to itself
                herein I'm happy to be
          contained though sometimes enough
                the cosmos isnt big
                but pressing in on me
        and measuring the tenderness that binds
      us all together yes Daedalus that word that sacred word
                which is so hard to say
              when hearts wear all this skin
              and numb bone in between
              drives bargains with the devil
                        yet
              turn it twist and go on heel
            to visit the land of the sun womb
            where warm in its mercy you suckle
                the tube with the food in

          but other things had she in mind for my mind
              she had other things on her mind

                          o
                        city
                      at night
                      I'm yours
                        and
                    all my children
                    still unborn
                        lie in
                the peace you know today
                  so slight and sweet
                    and yet to be

He went to the french windows and tapped at the door.
Frances pulled the curtain back, unlocked them and let him in.
She looked fierce about something and the room went quiet as
he entered. Barbara was queening it over him with her eyes
                      i been hoodood
                      i been voodood

A Day at the Office

«So you enjoyed your beer did you?» Frances pierced at him with her eyes.

«Yes thanks.»

«And you've finally consented to come in? To grace us with your presence.»

whazgoinonin here

Barbara and Hilda were waiting with their coats

ah

«Well Douglas, it's been nice seeing you again dear. I'd have loved to hear something more about the gallery but perhaps next time. Maybe while Barbara's here, you'll come over and have dinner some evening?»

grinbear

«Yes, sometime ... »   noncommital

grenadier

«And of course we're expecting an invitation to the opening.»

Douglas fumbled hopelessly for words

«It's a way off yet.»

stalling

«That is if you want people with the money to buy there at all. Perhaps your art is more the kind that protests, but cant sell?» Hilda laughed,

she
was working that one out
from earlier
all rehearsed
and they laugh
why cant I speak

He kissed the cheek she offered, humbled.

«Of course I'll be delighted to see you there, Hilda.»

Barbara stepped forward, took his hand and squeezed it hard

hidden from the mother's eye on their blind side

«Douglas, dont you worry you'll be seeing more of me.»

Her eyes in the lenses of her glasses looked huge, bouncing with vitality and fun

I melt
away

The procession to the front door began.

After Hilda and Barbara had left, Douglas and his mother went into the kitchen. Douglas was drunk but wouldnt stay

the night despite her persuasion. All she could do was warn him
>saying

«You're a grown man now, responsible for your own actions. I cant make you do anything anymore.»

He had the feeling that this was an overture to something.

«You'll at least stay and have some coffee before you drive?»

He shrugged, nodded. «Yes, thanks.»
>presentiment
>something coming up

For years, every move he had made was subject to her scrutiny, and if she didnt like what she saw, she would soon tell him
>grimly governing with gloved hand
>a mother thatcher

The situation had changed with the inheritance. Although he knew it wasnt the sole factor in the change. It had taken time for them both to get over Hugh's death
>yet
>she still holds the reins
>it isnt mine yet

She clasped her hands and glowered at him for a few seconds, showing her displeasure, then changed her tack. She made them coffee, and they sat down at the kitchen table with a plate of shortbread. Once there, she stirred in a tablet of sweetener.

«Who is this girl, Douglas?»

He snorted in amusement
>she so predictable
>her little manouevres dont change
>same line at fifteen
>re the she

«Yes, I know all about it,» she said with a regal smile.

«Barbara told me while you were out in the garden.»

«I might have known,» he said, quietly.

«Not that it's any of my business, I suppose. You're old enough now to live your own life, as I say.»

Then she gave him a loving, maternal look.

«But Douglas, why didnt you tell me? I'm very interested to meet her. Helen, isnt it? What does she do? Where is she from?»

A Day at the Office

He felt himself sink into someone else, someone he had been once, years before.

«Do you remember Stuart Orr?»
or orr

The name conjured ghosts. Hugh stirred in their collective memory,
wrapped in swaddling bandages
grossly old and infant merged

«I had hoped I would never hear that name again,» she said, almost inaudibly. It was as he had thought. It was still very much alive for her.»

«Helen is Stuart's sister.»

She froze, stiff, her eyes glazed over. It was a full minute before she could speak. Finally there came a kind of whining noise that turned into his name
pleading

«Douglas. I dont understand. Why are you doing this to me?»

«To you? What do you mean?»
not

«Reminding me. Bringing it all up again. Why on earth, of all the female members of the human race, have you got involved with Stuart Orr's sister? Dont you remember what he did to your brother? What is the matter with you? Is this some kind of game?»

Her voice rose till it reached the brink of hysteria. He put his hand on her arm.

«Easy, Mum.»
with eyessay
who can ever choose
where the heart leads us

She stared at him blankly. It was many months since he had last called her Mum.

«Do you still see him?» she asked, as if afraid of an affirmative response.

«Now and again.»

She got up from the table and walked across the room to the window. For a long time, she stood looking out, with her back to him. He sighed, lit and smoked a cigarette.

«Why?» she asked but not of him. She was staring at the Japanese print of the setting sun
or is it east and rising now

The light seemed thin and incapable of penetrating beyond her silhouette. Yes it had taken time for them to get over Hugh. But the estate existed and there was no doubt it was now an obstacle between them, preventing them from forming bonds directly, turning their relationship into a business partnership
in which they were both restlesssleepers
It was difficult at times. But it could not realistically be otherwise. As long as he kept himself separate in
my own world
his own individual space, everything worked fine. Even if she didnt approve of the way he used his money, it was his sooner or later
a solitary heir
Tonight had reaffirmed the decision he had made three years ago.

He would not return to that pale world to live, but had found the sun to be elsewhere from this
this dinner party world
«It's coincidence, that's all,» he said, but
dont really believe that does one?
She sighed and turned back to face him.

«Douglas, I meant what I said earlier.»

«Oh? What was that?»

«About my being concerned about you?»

«Oh? Why?» He nibbled from a piece of shortbread.

«Well I dont really want to pry, but today while I was in town I went into the bank
and yes yes I know
and I was talking to Mr Graham. He just happened to mention that he has written to you a number of times asking you to go to see him and that you havent even bothered to reply.»

«I see. What else did he say?»
how much do you know
She moved closer, stared at him, her eyes tender and requiring reciprocation
from me me me
«If you've got yourself into difficulties, I think I have the right to know at least. Or have you forgotten the money I loaned to you?»

«No I havent forgotten that. And you'll be pleased to know

that everything is in hand and I expect to repay you within the month. And the bank too.»

«But how, dear? We're not talking about a few hundred pounds now are we?»

«I have a deal pending which is going to make more than enough.»

His tone of voice was firm and seemed to reassure her a little, despite what she had said.

«Well why dont you just go and explain that to Mr Graham? If there's really no problem with it, then just let him know. I mean you really should have security for a loan of that size. I know that it's perhaps not a large amount of money in comparison with the extent of the estate, but nevertheless, it's important to remember that there are certain rules of conduct. Ways of doing business.»

say nothing hope it'll slide
seconds passing
now
now

«Well are you going to tell me?»

«What?»

«What you've done with the money?»

Her face had lost its tenderness, there was no covering expression but worry and it was

not directed only to me
say
wait

«Just wait. You'll see. It will all work out just fine.»

«The time for assurances has passed, surely? Dont you agree that perhaps something a bit more concrete is called for?»

«It's.»

come come
not a thing that I can do
think think

« ... well a surprise I suppose.»

«Oh?»

not sufficient

« ... well I suppose if I have to explain I will. It's your Peploe.»

o horrorlie

Frances Shaw was shocked at first, then smiled and sat

back, breathless. A smile spread over her face.

«You mean?»

«I mean your Peploe. I met someone in London who thinks that he can buy it for me. I had to provide him with the necessary funds, but he's a reputable dealer and a friend besides. He's in Amsterdam right now.»

«I see ... »

> it's working
> working
> but oh that horrorlie

«I didnt want to mention it to Graham in case he told you. It was to be a surprise.»

> three times the horror lie

She was delighted. He could see that.

«Well of course he is a dreadful gossip I know.»

«I cant make any promises about the painting yet, but if my friend cant deliver, the money will be returned.»

She nodded, as if understanding all. It was perhaps irregular, but then so very very kind of him.

The story worked as he hoped it would, and even though he hated having to tell it, he had prepared it some time before. It was clear that she was quite thrilled that he should have been so thoughtful. There were no more questions. Her eyes welled with tears.

«You know dear, I'm touched. Truly. But you know, the painting isnt that important to me. Oh I know I made a lot of it at the time, but then that was before, you know. After Hugh ... it was just as well, I sometimes think, that he sold it. Otherwise, if, you know, I'd still had it, I would ... »

> she without words

«What I want more than anything is for our lives to be bright again. I want the sun to shine, Douglas. Goodness knows we've had enough cloud on our horizon.»

Her hand reached across the table to take cover his. He was

> freeze framed

«But this Helen, I just want to know, she isnt ... »

«What?»

«Involved with drugs?»

Douglas grinned. He could tell the truth.

«No. Not at all.»

«Because you know if I ever thought you were still involved

in that world, I'd lose all sense of reason, really. You've no idea what it would do to me.» She was crying
                    yes crying
                    a small tear
                    but still one

«Oh I know you've blamed me. I know you thought I drove Hugh away. But I've suffered for that. One day you'll understand. You'll have children of your own. Then you'll understand ... »

She let go his hand and stood up, recovering her composure. Douglas leaned back in his chair. The lie
                    the horrorlie
                    echoed

and i have seen life tonight
have listened to
a hundred plus
opinions
on the many issues
currently in vogue
ALL ROUNDED UP AND RATIONALISED
IT MAKES A TIDY PILE OF PLASTIC
IN THE TV COMPANY FILE
a record of our time
the voice of our time
a sign of our time
the cause of our time
view and counterview
a tale of lust and greed
of passion's thrusting hand
and what it grips
LANGUAGE GOUGING MEMORY
MUSIC GAUGING HOPE

there's
no such thing as harmless
fantasy
if it was harmless
no one would want it
JUST LEARN TO BE GRATEFUL
FOR OFFICIAL RELEASE
switch off the lightning
the moon is

u
p

above the speckled city
a mist descends upon the valley
the crane returns
to its rooftop roost
the red car turns
into a bay mare
is parked in the cul-de-sac

A Day at the Office

encourage
s l e e p d r e a m

Ray lay in bed in the dark. He was stoned and his head was spinning with strange thoughts that were
       so gorgeous that I couldnæ bear to miss them

He had taken the ghetto blaster through to his room and had plugged his headphones in. He didnt like leaving it lying around when Erchie was about. Not that he'd nick it or anything, but he might just wreck it if he was drunk
      or pawn it if he was hard up

Today was his giro day. Ray knew the pattern of his movements well. He'd be up early, washed and shaved before the post, then down to the Post Office to cash it, and have a bacon and egg breakfast before hitting the White Hoose.

For the rest of the day, he'd be nipping between there and the bookies, then maybe get a supper and head for the Thistle Club. By this time, most of the cash would be gone, barring that he'd backed a miracle
      on four legs

It was weird. He'd been out of work for eight years, but he still looked on giro day as payday, like he did each Friday when he was working. A man deserves a night out
      after a week's graft
      that was the thing
      the endless pattern of macho movement

When the tape side finished, Ray nipped the j, and put it on his saucer ashtray for morning. The toothache was nagging and getting to sleep was tough, even stoned. He was just entering slumberland when he heard the door open. It was him, kind of mumbling and singing to himself, like he was happy. Maybe he'd got a winner after all. Ray heard him rumbling about the kitchenette, then it fell quiet. Half asleep, stoned dreaming, he sensed the smell of curry drifting through the house
      mixing with the beer in the stomach
      he'll be
      an oor in the bog in the mornin
      old rot gut

      slippin

        driftin

        smell

        driftin

        driftin

He began to
                flicker picker
                luck and maybe
                that was what
          it would be when it came to
           be the chance to get
           out from under Kathy
           who's this guy with
           the gear stick maybe
            changin into him
            and getting smart
            suit car CD ETC ooh
            that music mozart
            the most art but
her that Brenda was she not the bizz buzz best that

      it would I half a chance to be

         really there their

            where

          the heart is

             drift

             away
         wanna get lost

        gimme the beat
             man

A Day at the Office

>free my soul

>ole man river
>deliver

>me from temptation
>till mornin

>comes

His eyes shut and the sleep if it had dreams in it, they
>passed
>under
>the bridge
>unkent

When Ray woke up, the sun was up and he tuned in the radio to get the time, tuned into house music, doctor in the house

>doctorin the house?
>doc tore in the house?
>good mornin peeps
>it's eightthirtyeight
>and you're listenin to
>radio one
>and that was Yazz
>with her plastic peeps

Ray got up and went to the kitchen. He was only wearing his ys and the flat was

>freezin

cold. He put the kettle on and went back to the warmth of his sleeping bag. Lyin there cosy the

>stiffness

>absorbs all

>scratching and rubbing

>awaking

>that Brenda

>was gorgeous

>a doll man

a doll

but alive too

with skin man

and hair

and that arse

and there's no point in

thinkin

i cant have her can i

she's only a woman

she real man

you know her

just phone her

invite her

a date her

and later

you'll make her

do that o o oh

The kettle was boiling. He could hear it hissing. He got up and went to the bog, washed himself down and looked at himself in the mirror. He looked okay, like today might work out fine, he felt as if he could do it, make things happen. He hopped quickly through into the kitchen
        feeling oozed soothe
        smoothed
Erchie was snoring on the couch in the living room. He had taken his shoes off and the place really stunk of sweaty feet. Almost
        boakin bolkin

A Day at the Office

Ray crossed to the windows and opened them both wide. The air was crisp and clear and the rain of yesterday was gone. Holding his nose he went back out, closing the door on the stink, the
filthy old fucker
never washes
pig man
He found a half clean shirt and socks and got dressed. He drank a mug of tea bag
t

and smoked   a wee spliff
something's happening
i'm in the middle of it at last
and   want to get moving
wait no more
i
thought   let's go
go

He began to sort out all his belongings. A few clothes, a few books, a few tapes
what else is there
but books and records of our time
like
dont forget
Alex Harvey
play it
He put the old scratched record on the old wrecked stereo
kid memories of crying
when Alex was dying
just as
i wanna be rich and famous
i wanna be just the same as
the stars that shine on the chrissymas tree
chorus

Ray had packed up everything he wanted to take with him. The room was bare, no longer his, and now contained only the faintest trace of all the time he had spent in it. He opened the window and stood for a moment looking down. From the sixth floor, the hump of earth in the middle of the five blocks looked green, and the concrete circle around it seemed clean.

Some kids were playing there
the lucky on their bikes
their shouts carried up to his ear, they must have been
dumped out early
happy, totally in place there, among the dogshit and the

broken glass.
   As he had been, not so long past, among them
                       weights made of lead
                       hangin round my heart
The blocks of flats were like
                           guardians
                         rigid shepherds
                       watchin oer the flock
                          but uncaring
                         bad husbands
and now that he was leaving, he felt there was some reason for all this building. He
                  got sentimental over you
imagined himself for a few minutes
                         one of the kids
                   cycling round and round
                       the muddy mound
                          rutting tracks
But the guardians all faced the city centre, and shepherded the kids away from the cornfields which enclosed Eastercraigs from the south. The guardian eyes focussed on the empty castle, five miles away to the north. The direction Ray was headed. Once the bikes were discarded there was no other way but that
                              hope
He turned away from the window and sat on his bed. The mattress was uncovered and it felt damp. For some reason the night of his mother's funeral came to mind, when he and Erchie and Gordon sat up late drinking whisky together, till the boozing tongues got careless and the air got tight with threats
                          of doings
                          punchup
Ray had hardly seen the old guy since then. The heavy depression which hung around the flat made him avoid it as much as he could. The old woman used to say they brought out the worst in each other. But all the same, he felt like he should wait before he left and say cheerio to the old guy. For his maw's sake maybe.
   So he loitered a while, rolled a j and smoked it hanging out the window, watching the kids go round and round. The bareness of the room had a liberating effect on his mind
                          time passed

A Day at the Office

idling
remembering
hot city

He peeped into the living room. Erchie was still crashed, but the smell was bearable at least. He began poking about in drawers in the units, looking for nothing in particular but driven by the notion that this might be the last time he would have the chance to.

He found the old sweetie tin that had the family photos in it. He decided to take a few with him. He could probably have taken the whole box, Erchie wouldnt care but he didnt want to

just a few
select few

there were lots of her family, people he'd never met. They all lived somewhere up north

if there was any of them still that is

His maw had been pregnant with him, with no father to be seen. They had packed her off to stay with cousins here when the thing happened

so no too many tongues wag
that was me
i ray
allegeditimate
baby me
look at this wan man
see that double Carnation milk chin
næ teeth
but happy wee chap me then
what was the place again
Harta or somethin
island was it

For the first time in a long time, Ray asked the question where

did i come from

He gathered a small pile of photos, mainly of himself and his mother. There was one of their wedding

Erchie solider smart soldierlike
than ever i mind him

Erchie stirred on the couch, grunted and turned over, then opened one eye and stared at Ray. He didnt speak for a while. Ray picked up the pile of photos he was taking, stuck them in his pocket and closed the tin. Erchie gave a loud snort, like he couldnt breathe properly.

–Ray, he grunted. He almost seemed pleased to see him. –

No seen you for weeks son.
 –Months even, Ray answered. –I've just come back to pick up a few things. I'm moving into a flat up the toon.
 –It's helluva cold in here, can you no close thæ windæs?
 –I only opened them cos o your feet.
 –Whit's the matter wi my feet?
 –They're fucking stinkin, that's whit.
 –Are they? He sniffed at the socks. –God you're right.
But he didnt move to do anything about it.
 –I was just lookin through these photos. Thought I might take a few.
 Erchie snorted again. –Take what you want son. I never look at them. I got my memories up here. He tapped his temple with a forefinger. Then he leaned over towards Ray.
 –Got a fag there son, I'm oot till I go tæ the shop.
 Ray took out his tobacco tin and tossed it over to him where he lay stretched out on the pvc settee. The good one his maw had bought had gone to the secondhand shop a while ago, for this old shit and some cash, and the cash had gone to the bookies.
 As he caught it, Ray said –Skint then?
 Erchie grinned. –Naw. As a matter of fact, I had a wee bit luck wi a pony. I'm flush,- he said, then –Whit is it, you needin a sub son?
 Ray realised
                       why the old guyso pleased lookin
But watching him roll the cigarette, he thought how he was still the same
                            old reptile
                   the same hard scabby face
      that wee pink tongue poking in and out as he licked the paper
 Erchie glanced up from the operation without raising his chin.
 –So where's this flat then?
 Ray knew what would happen if he gave him the address. Next time he was skint, he'd be up there looking to tap him for a tenspot till the giro came.
 –Up at Blacklins.
 –Blacklins? Bit snobby roond there, is it no?
 Ray just shrugged. Erchie straightened up on the settee, and leant forward, fag in mouth, to put his shoes on.

—You're right enough about these socks, he said, then leaned back and signalled Ray to pass his matches.

—They're honkin, Ray suggested.

—Aye. There was something about his expression that was saying
> i want nothin fæ you son

—Make yoursel a cuppæ tea, Ray.

Ray pointed to an empty mug at his feet. —I just had one.

Erchie sighed. —Och I'll make one mysel, he muttered and rose up to go through to the kitchenette. He called through to Ray above the sound of the tap rushing water.

—So are you workin then, son?

Ray shouted back —No. No the now.

Erchie re-emerged, drying his hands on a crumpled dishtowel.

—Same old story, eh? he said, flinging the towel down on the arm of his chair.
> but naw
> it goes much farther than that

There was all that time between them since the old girl had died. There was the state of their voided relationship. The barriers of mistrust and dislike that had been softened by his mother now seemed insurmountable
> but
> even the Berlin Wall can fall
> and
> time might alter anything

On his side of the wall, Ray could not imagine liking Erchie or even pitying him sufficiently at some future point when he might be infirm, in
> dote age

That was the way it was, though he could remember a time when things had been different, when
> i wanted a father
> believed Erchie might be
> but that was maw's work
> mediator
> excludin herself so we could be together
> twas alright while the match was on
> but when the whistle blew
> we found we were shoutin for different teams
> maybe she had overdone it
> maybe she had tried too hard to push us together

and had only pushed us apart
maybe may be
but all that was done with anyway

Erchie brought Ray a cup of tea, unasked for. Ray took it.

−Thanks.

Erchie put on the tv
some chat show discussion prog
talking about child abuse
did he
hit me
no mind it
repressed
no couldnt be surely
no a bad old guy
is he

Ray looked at his watch. There would be a bus in five minutes, at the terminus. He got up to go towards the door. Erchie got quite agitated.

−So you're away then?

−Well I'm ready.

−Are you comin back then? More stuff to collect like?

−Naw. I've got all I want, Erch.

−But you'll be back?

Ray shrugged, picked up his bags, took hold of the door handle. As he did so Erchie edged in front of him. They stood there in a sort of half embrace, Ray's hand on the handle, between Erchie's side and arm. Boozy breath covered the side of Ray's head, as he gave the door a tug.

Æ ...

Ray frowned. −What is it, Erchie? I got to go.

His stepfather moved out of the way, the door stood ajar, revealing the dark hall behind. Erchie rubbed his stubbled chin.

Æm ...

Ray sniffed and moved towards the door again, just as Erchie did the same. They bumped into each other and Ray got angry.

−Whit is this, a fuckin dance or somethin?

He waited. Erchie turned away from the door and walked briskly across the room to the units. He opened a door and took something out.

−If you're no comin back, son, you'd best take this. She

asked me to gie it you before she died. I was going to that night after the funeral, but ... ach you ken whit happened.

He held out a closed fist and Ray opened his hand. Erchie dropped a small gold locket into his palm. Ray nodded, looked at it a minute, then closed his fist around it
>
> it wasnæ worth much
> but at least he hadnæ sold it

–An there was something else, Erchie said. –That picture o hers. She said for you tæ hæ that.
>
> the photo of the island
> she wanted me
> to have it

Ray waited for Erchie to move but he didnt. He just stood there.

–Gonnæ get it yoursel, Ray? I dont like goin in there, son.
–In her room here?
–Aye.

Ray pushed the door open. He looked around him. Nothing had changed. Earlier, before Erchie woke, he had thought of going in there, but he hadnt done it.

The black and white photo of his mother's childhood home still hung above the dressing table. Ray had the image in his head
>
> a misty memory
> ages since i actually seen it

but he had forgotten exactly what it was like. Now he was lifting it from the wall, rubbing his sleeve over the glass, examining it
>
> this only connection with place of conception
> it's weird this weird
> a rocky landscape
> sea in the distance
> a few houses tucked into the hill
> no name obvious

There were a couple of damp spots now but its condition was good on the whole. Ray felt
>
> warm
> warm things

He was turning to leave when he saw another photo. It clicked a memory of being a kid, it was a picture of his mother when she was young. It had always intrigued him as a kid, for in it, she still had her own teeth. He could only remember her clearly with a perfectly straight set of dentures, but here her

smile revealed the teeth crooked and overlapping in places. And all of a rush came over him
>   her
>   smell
>   her voice
>   her
>   being
>   there
>   no more

He shivered. It was daft them leaving the room like that. They should have cleared it out. If there had been a ghost
>   i might have seen the point
>   but she was ready to die
>   she chose it when she started taking steroids
>   she knew they'd do her liver in
>   but she was tired of operations
>   hospitals and special diets
>   she had chosen to die
>   and so had left no ghost

Ray closed the bedroom door as he went out into the hall, carrying the photo
>   she wanted me to have

Erchie was peeping out of the living room.

−Did you get it?

−Aye. Ray held it up for him to see, then knelt down and unzipped one of his bags. He put the picture inside. Erchie seemed relieved, like his task was now complete.

−Righto, he said. Erchie stepped forward.

−Æm Ray, you couldnæ let me have a bit o that baccy æ? Save me nippin oot tæ the shop.

Ray grinned, brought out his tobacco tin as Erchie pulled out his pouch. They did the deal between them, transferring some of the precious weed from one to the other.

−Aye well, Erchie said, turning back inside the room. −Aw the best son.

Ray picked up his bags and opened the front door.

−See you sometime.

Ray went for the lift, which was out of order as usual. He started down the stairs.

The open air was welcome. He walked the hundred yards or so to the bus terminus, past the chipper, weighed down by the bags. But he was
>   finally doing it

                              finally goin
                            no idea where
                         but shawguys maybe
                               Janjoes
                       maybe Kathy lovely Brenda
                         maybe find that place
                              go north
He bought a ticket for fifty pence
                              outa here
piled his bags up in the space behind the driver's seat and sat down. Looking round at the blocks of flats behind him, he knew that this was final. He had been leaving for a long time, but this was it.

The driver checked his watch and started up the engine. The bus jerked forward, through the scheme and out onto the bypass, over the flyover, past the shopping centre, and away to the north. Every stop was an annoyance, he just wanted to go, straight on, with no time to think back or wonder.
He wanted
                       a chance to do something
                        tæ get oot and milk it
                          maybe even work

                        everything's up for review

> the world of dreams synthesised
> realities
> disparate
> the actual and the imaged
>
> after judgement day
> I ray
> no more
> now here
> in centre
> freed from the dreaming
> now become conscience
>
> **time curves loops returns
> to**

the time Douglas got back, it was after three
> Helen may well be asleep

He tried to make as little noise as possible going in but his key got stuck in the lock and when he pulled at it, it came with such a jerk he lost his balance. He swayed back, bumped into the hatstand and nearly knocked it over. He was drunker than he had realised
> did not know he was
> playing the fool
> for the world

Stepping lightly down the hall, trying to suppress the click of his shoes on the polished floorboards, he went into his bedroom. The curtains were open and the street lamp outside the window lit the empty bed. There was no sign of her. He thought for a moment, then went back to the stairs and up one storey to her flat.

«Helen? Are you in there?» There was no answer. He took a bunch of keys from his pocket and selected the master
> blaster

As the door swung open, he called again. There was no sound. No light.

«Helen?»

No reply.

He went into the lounge and switched the standing lamp on. In his head, there was a

                              fog
                       a dishonest fog
                     obscuring everything
He could take a line but didnt
                              want
His attitude was
                              changed
In lying
                              to mother
he had started to
                              lose myself

   The brick was not heavy. The brick was the lightest burden she could ever imagine carrying. It was
                       my stone of destiny.
                       represents integrity
                            of being
                           the legend
   As she climbed the steps, an operatic frenzy blaring out reached Helen's ears before she had even opened the street door. The music was coming from Douglas' flat, filling the whole stairwell with
                           dramatic
romance. His door was wide open, but there was no sign of any light. She knocked and called his name but the music was so loud, he couldnt possibly have heard her. Fumbling about in the hall, looking for the light switch, she tripped over something and fell, bruising her shinbone. It was that goddamned bicycle
                       why dont he dump it
                           never used
                       rubs make it better
   Standing up again, she got her hand on the switch, and turned the light on.
   'Douglas! Are you alright?' she called again, but there was no reply.
   The opera was reaching a crescendo and was drowning everything. She picked up the fallen bike, and set it up again, against the wall.
   As the music came to an end, she heard the sound of water running in the bathroom. The door was shut and she could see

no light through the glass. She knocked
                    tiptap
from inside
                splash
  'Douglas? Are you in there?' Water swilled about.
  'Are you alright?' She tried the door. It wasnt locked.
'Douglas?'
  She peeped round the door. A cigarette lighter clicked on, and in its
                    tiny orb of
light she saw him, grinning at her from the bath. He looked really wasted. 'I was shouting but you didnt answer,' she explained.
  'I heard you,' he replied, 'Wont you come in? There's a seat over there.'
  He pointed to the lavatory. Laughing, she put her things on the floor, and sat down. Douglas put a flame to a candle perched on the side of the bath
                    clever
                masterfireandwater
  'What's the idea?' she asked, 'Lying here in the dark like this?'
  He smiled. 'I wanted to try out that thinktank thing. You know, sensory deprivation,' he answered, then sank under the water and lay blowing bubbles up for a few seconds. When he reappeared, she asked 'Did it work?'
  He shook his head. 'Not well enough.'
  'Didnt you forget something?'
  'What?'
  'Your ears. I could hear that music in the street.'
  'That wasnt music, my dear, that was Wagner.'
                    Lohengrin
  She shook her head
                    scots it
  'Too Germanic for me, ken?'
  He submerged under a second frothy wave. For a moment, she saw him drowning, like his face was under
                not warm bath water
                but the cold river
she had stared into an hour before,
                like he's going under
                the bridge and out to sea

> an electric shock it's
> shrivelling
> superreal

When he came up, water streaming over his features, eyes tight shut, his mouth opened. He roared out 'FO ... OH' at the candle
> meaningless

breath blew it out. Then it was quiet and dark. Only the gentle swilling of the water and the hush from the amp in the lounge mixed.

'What's the matter?' she asked
> tell me

The lighter clicked and he lit the candle again, then glanced at her, making with an effort at a smile. He shook his head again but this time he was saying
> yes
> something's wrong
> I dont know what it is
> but I know it's wrong
> finally

there were words.

'I went to my mother's today. I went to dinner there. I got drawn in, you know, into the whole
> petty

mess. Her world.'

Helen said nothing. She was thinking
> let it go
> let it go
> letigo

'Did she say something to you?'
'It's just all that stuff about proper conduct, you know.'
He looked
> totally exasperated

'Was it your brother again?'
He slapped his hand down on the water surface gently, causing a few tiny bubbles to rise into the
> steamy   air

'No, not that, not this time. Though I suppose his ghost's there all the time, in the house, even if we dont talk about him'.
'Dont you? I mean, talk about him?'
'No.'
She sighed
> end of conversation

'Do you want a towel? Or should I go?'
He sat up quickly. 'No, stay, please, Helen. I'd like to talk.'
He meant it. She looked around the bathroom. 'In here?'
'Why not?'
She leaned back against the cistern. She knew she could help him. She knew
<pre>
                            exactly
what he needed. He was
                     totally naked here
                       transparent
                           but
                       soaking wet
                      full of poison
                           stiff
                      appealing to her
She could heal him take the ache away
                     aware of myself
                    vaguely I stand up
                    take off my coat
                    slip off my shoes
      unzip my trousers and let them fall to the floor
                    pull off my sweater
                          socks
                         branicks
                 strip myself slowly naked
                       to be like him
                      while he watches
                      his face half in
                          shadow
                         uncertain
</pre>
'What's going on?' he breathed
<pre>
                          quietly
                        half smiling
</pre>
Unclothed, she turned away to
<pre>
                      set the brick stone
                         in position
</pre>
and stepped into the bath, put a foot either side of his legs then squatted down in the water, holding his eye with her stare, till she felt the water over
<pre>
                         my belly
</pre>
She leaned back until her head rested between the two taps, till
<pre>
                         my nipples
</pre>
touched the soapy water surface. Douglas' erection poked like a dolphin's head through the bubbles.

'We are in this thing together,' she said solemnly, like she was a character in some thriller
we laugh a
little
but aches me it's
not to be filled
rightnow
as
the moonth wanes
She looked away from him, broke eye contact. She glanced at the nearby toilet pan, with velvet toilet seat cover, on which her brick stood
proudly
bearing the legend of L E N N O X.
'Well? What do you think of my stone of destiny?'

Douglas laughed, he could not
that
self stop
so
earthy
«It's wonderful.»
«You like it?»
«Of course.»
i
«You really mean that, right?»
d
«I said so, didnt I.»
o
Helen nodded. «Good.»
«Because wherever I go from now on, that brick goes with me, right?» She laughed. Her tone was humorous but
she seems to mean it
«I love your brick, ok?»
She turned to him
quizzically
«You do know where that is, dont you?»
«Lennox? Of course. I've been there.»
«How many times?»
«Oh I dont know. Two or three maybe.»
She lifted her chin a fraction and let it drop

      a no d

Helen was thinking
     this water around me
   is warming so soothing the back pain
   and what's it he's crucified over
     this pretty boy
     is he tellin truth
'You never told me much about Hugh, you know. When I asked you that time, you were very short with me.'
 'I just want to put it in the past, Helen.'
 'But if it's still eatin you up inside, you've got to do something about it.'
 'There nothing eatin me up inside, except money.'
 'Money?' She genuinely couldnt
      quite grasp that
 'Did you say money? Have you any idea how poor some people are?'
 'You dont understand, this isnt my money, it's business. It's somebody else's money.'
 'Oh.'
    no he's lost somebody else's money
     has he cant have
      sighs
'I'm sorry for snapping, Helen. And by the way I should have said, it's not my money yet. I should have said that.'
She shrugs. 'It's ok.'
      irish it
'Sure you've got your problems too.'
      but he
      no smile
     is he thinking

       if
      she asks
       poetry
      that word
     if she but asks it
«Can I help?»
«Maybe.»

A Day at the Office

«How?»
«Just listen to me. I want to tell you about me.»
«You mean you want therapy?»
«No. I just want to tell you what I'm like, really»
She hesitated.
I fill it with voice
«I feel like I need to confess. As if I've committed a heinous crime
like a felon
«As if I've done something tonight that will change the course of my life.»
Her eyes
brightening
gleam
«Well I am a lapsed Catholic.»
He looked at her and could see that it would be safe to tell, yet couldnt bring himself to begin. He stood up in the bath, and picked up a towel. The water was running off
me
He was about to turn and go when she spoke.
«You had a visitor today?»
«Oh? Who was that?»
«A woman called Barbara something or other.»
«Barbara Gilmour?»
the hell
of course
that's how knew
«What did she want?»
«Oh, just nosing, I think. She said you'd invited her to look round the gallery.»
«Did she indeed? I hope you didnt let her in.»
«Should I not have?»
no but
burnt fingers
gingerly
«Barbara is exactly the kind of person I wanted to get away from when I moved in here.»
«Well I did let her in. But she didnt stay long. I kept her nose at arms length. We had a drink of your whisky.»
beautiful
she
«Though she was surprised to see me there.»

«Yes, I'm sure she would have been. Barbara's idea of world affairs is who's sleeping with who. And it didnt take her long to get the news that I've got a live-in spread all the way back to my mother's.»

Helen raised herself onto her elbows. «Does that matter?»

«No, of course not. It's just that it might cause problems. She tries to interfere so much.»

likes digging
Frances does

«You know I really want to meet this woman, your mother. This Frances. From what you've told me, and the impression Barbara gave me, she sounds quite a lady.»

she is she is
but keep distance
you
dont know
how she feels about
Stuart Helen

«Do you want some more hot water in?»

«I'm getting out anyway»

step out
drip down

He began rubbing himself with a fish-patterned bathtowel, glanced down at her.

«But thanks, you've solved one puzzle for me already.»

«Have I?»

«Yes. And I'm going to go and fetch you another whisky as a reward.»

«Oh dont bother. I'd rather have a cup of tea. Or just come and talk some more. You said you wanted me to therapise you. You havent told me what it is you've done that's so terrible yet.»

what have I done
how to in words describe
the deed of killing motherlove

«I have lifted someone's expectations up so high ... »

He opened up his arms to sign the widest space he could. «And just let them down. I havent got a hope of doing what I said I might.»

does that say it
not how I feel

Helen shrugged, wagged her head from side to side
rapidly

A Day at the Office

    with an expression of
>not impressed

  «Och people do that all the time, it's called bluffing,» she said.
    Douglas frowned
>if she's teasing me
>walk out

She smiled not unkindly.
  «Dont be so soft.»

    Douglas walked out of the bathroom. Helen felt a bit ashamed for being so unsympathetic. But he didnt deserve sympathy
>carry ongoing like he did

She was concerned, but not swayed, by his act, lay back in the bath and thought of staying there forever. There was nothing now could penetrate her, now that she had found the brick and the integrity that went along with it
>like
>stone of destiny
>a piece of
>jacob's pillow
>brought by scoti
>who travelling on from thrace
>passed through judæa
>stole a piece of holy stone
>the black meteorite
>to carry it north through
>africa
>gibraltar
>iberia
>to ireland
>dalriada

It was
>the stone which makes
>the temple
>home
>crypt
>i want to be a bungalow
>and decorate it for my tomb

she thought
>with cats and carpets
>cars and couches

                    with gold and silver paint
                            with love
                               yet
                           there are
                     patterns and earrings
                 different ways of dancing singing
                 butter for the scones and always tea

  Douglas was in the kitchen and the kettle was boiling when
Helen came through dressed in a robe, and sandals on her feet.
She looked
                           at home here
                           a part of me
  «Would you like some toast?»
                              ask I
  «Mmmm ... mm.»
                           singing voice
  She sat at the table
                        the old oaken table
  and picked up the cat's
                      empty   basket.
  «When was it your cat disappeared again?»
                       filling teapot toast in
  «About two months ago.»
  «Just before I moved in?»
  «When was that again? It seems longer than that.»
  «November the fourteenth.»
  «It was about Halloween, I think. I remember it was the
fireworks, I thought perhaps that had scared her. Why?»
  «Just wondered that's all.»
                       cat go girl come
                           easy easy
                     toast browned this side
  «So where's your brick then? I thought you said it was
going to go everywhere with you from now on.»
  «I put it to bed. It was tired.»
  «Ah.»
                      let sleeping bricks lie
                               lie
                          horror down
                             Peploe
                  a name I'll never speak again

«Helen,»
>					toast out
>					get cups

«How would you feel about someone else taking the flat upstairs?»
>					flares

Incredulous she enquires «my flat?»

«Well you hardly use it any more. It's just that I met this young lad today, I really took to him. He's quite desperate for somewhere to stay.»

«And you told him he could have my flat, is that what you're saying?»
>					my god you read me
>					too well

«I ... ah,» Douglas stammered, a little taken aback at her sharpness.

«No, I didnt make any promises, I just ... » He shuffled his feet. «Felt sorry for him. I thought you'd really like him, actually.»

«What, two strays together?»

She stood up and marched to the door.

«Let me tell you that's my flat and I dont want to give it up. Ok?»

Then she exited
>					slamming door
>					clear
>					if ray coming helen out

She shouted down from the hall outside.

«I dont want your toast. And I dont want you.»

>					wait
>					long minutes
>					quivering
>					drink whisky
>					before

He went upstairs to her flat. The door was locked. He called but no one answered. So he took out the master key and let himself in. Looking into the bedroom, he saw her curled up under the covers. He went in and sat down on the edge of the bed. She was awake, lying there staring into space.

«What do you want, Douglas?»

«You,» he joked. «I want you.»

She turned onto her back and looked at him. «Leave me alone, Douglas, please.»

«What's the matter? Are you feeling alright?»

«Yes, of course. I just want to be on my own and think.»

«Are you sure you're not angry? I really didnt make any promises, Helen.»

She shook her head.

«I told you, I'm not mad.»

He took her hand which was lying on the bed cover
open palm
«Then what's the matter?»

With an impatient snort, she pulled her arm away from him. «For chrissake, does something have to be the matter for me just to want to lie here in my own bed and think?»

Douglas said nothing. Even in the dim light, it was clear that she was annoyed. The outline of her face in profile, glistening in the yellow lamplight,
is the shape of a frown
He looked at her for a moment, then shook his head, and leant forward to kiss her. She twisted away from him.

«You're stinking of booze,» she complained, then lay back down on her pillow.

Douglas stretched out his hand and stroked her shoulder.

«You look so beautiful lying there,» he said
softly
«You're drunk.» She responded to his attempted caress by shifting across the bed.

«What is it now?» he asked.

She sighed deeply. «Nothing,» then she raised herself up again.

«But I was thinkin, before you came in just now, about you having all the things that you do. Being, you know, well off.»

«You dont know the half of it.»

«Probably not. But I'd like to know, Douglas, really I would do.»

She rolled her head slowly round, signalling the space that he owned
that I live in
«I mean I cant imagine what it is to own not just your own

A Day at the Office

home but other people's too. To have control over their space, to be able to give them what they need. To be able to
be
bene
ficient
influence other people's lives like that. It's like it's ... »
she hesitates
for lack of wordage
for fear of hurt

«What?»

«It's too much power for one person to wield.»

«Tenants do have rights you know. It's not as if landlords can do what they like.»

She sneered. «Dont you mean 'we'?»

Douglas resisted getting drawn in further. She was mad
no question
about that
She tossed her head and turned away, then looked back
accusingly
«It's like you coming marching in here, after I've locked the door.»

Douglas protested.

«I didnt know if you were in. You didnt answer. If you'd told me to go away, I would have.»

«But you're missing the point. The point is you do have that key, that fucking master key. Fuckin master.» She glared at him
jumpin master
withering his ego
He threw the keys on the bed next her.

«You know, you make me suffer,» he said, with a slight grin on his face, then chuckled
oomble oob
«But anyway, it's different between us.»

«Oh? How?»

In an attempt at a French accent, he grunted,

«We are lovers, chérie»

and tried to lean forward to kiss her. She pushed him away.

«That's not the point. This is my space here. If the rent's paid it's mine. Ok? You cant make any decisions about it till I stop paying rent. Right?»

He nodded
>I held his eye
>he nodded
>I believe him

'We are so different you know. From different worlds. You maybe dont see it but I do.'
>saith I
>in faith

He answered. 'I hadnt thought about it till tonight but youve no idea what I'm really like. I dont think I knew myself.'
>know thyself
>physician

He pulled off his shoes and lay down on the bed next to her, then half rolled on top of her.

'I cant,' she said. 'I've got back pains,'

But he didnt want to talk anymore, he wanted to
>kiss her
>stroke her
>ultimately
>love her

She signed disinterest by her eye
>the stone rolls away

and he lay on his back.

She said, 'Tell me about your family, Douglas.'
He tutted reluctance but she was
>determined

'No, I really want to know. You've hardly told me anything about them yet. Please. I really think it's important.'

He was staring up at the ceiling, thinking
>how did I get all this
>privilege
>an accident of birth

A Day at the Office

                  too simple surely
«Go on tell me,» she urged.

He said, 'It's really very boring.'
                  he said
'I suppose you could just say it was a tale of greed, spread over a few generations of a Scottish family, till it gets down to me and living off the fat of the land. But that would be too simple.'
                  concede it
He said, 'Are you sure you really want to know?'
                  I say
'I wouldnt be asking if I didnt.'

«Well, my great-grandfather, James Shaw came from somewhere down near Alloway, Burns country. He was a cabinet maker, a good one. He opened his own business, in the shop down below. My grandfather, Douglas, who I'm called after, he expanded into interior decoration. They had a rich merchant clientele. At that time, this Blacklands was just a tiny village round the cross. A community of Flemish weavers, actually, who had come over to Scotland some time in the seventeenth century and set up shop here. Canaan they called it.
«Are you sure about this?»
                  she nods
«Then the old aristocratic family, who owned the estate of Blacklins, you know the big house, it's a hospital now, they went bankrupt. The estate was sold off in bits to developers. My grandfather Douglas sold up his business and went into property. He and a cousin of his. They built half of Blacklands. All the old tenements from here to the foot of Torry Hill.
«The family fortune was thus made.»
                  she yawns
«I told you it was boring.»
«I'm just tired. What time is it?»

He stretched to see his watch under the soft light of the bedside lamp.
«Ten to four.»

She said, 'No, it isnt boring at all. But I didnt really mean your family finances, more just about the people, you know, you and your parents. Your brother.'
He said, 'That's even worse. You'd never believe it. Or even if you did, I dont think I would.'
'But dont you think it's good to talk about it. Get it out in the open air, come to see it for what it really is?'
She leaned in close to him. Her nose was merely a fraction from his. She could feel his breath upon her face.
'Can people change, Helen? I mean really, fundamentally. Not just their outward appearance. I think I need to know that it is possible. I need to believe that it can be done. You know I'm so wrapped up in things you wouldnt even believe possible. I feel like I've been living someone else's life. Like you ask me, what it is to be who I am, but I'm not that person, I'm not myself. I'm living for other people, doing things they want me to or at least what I imagine they want me to. I need to know that it's possible to live a life without all that. That I can do the right things. Make the right choices.'
She could feel him breathing heavily, trying to make the breath say what he wanted it to, trying to form words and meanings out of it.
'Do you know what I think? I think you should learn to relax. You dont have to prove anything. You're not your brother, not even his keeper. I think you should forget about him, and think about you and me. We could go anywhere, do anything. Something useful.'

Her expression was bland
                supercilious
not tender as he wanted it to be. She was speaking to him, telling him her thoughts, yet it seemed she told him nothing of

A Day at the Office

herself. What was she really thinking? Her eyes were wide open, full of twinkling humour, yet she was totally impenetrable. He had the feeling she was toying with him.

    Helen smiled
                       there has to be hope
'The world has changed. Think about the Berlin Wall. Think about the future, about the planet. You know that our children, I mean our generations, of course, they're going to ask us one day, what was it like when you were young, what did you do? Weve got to find some kind of answer. We have got to stop being kids. Really leave home, all that goes with it, the good and the bad. We have to grow up. We cant go on taking refuge in booze or dope or fantasy, not while the planet chokes to death.'
She rolled over on top of him.
'My bed,' she whispered. 'My bed tonight.'
                 to sleep
                 baby
                 sleep

    She felt heavy. He breathed in.
                    tense up these muscles
                            relax
«Am I heavy?» she asked him.

'You're acting strange' he said.
                      she whispers

'I am to you.'
                    but not to myself

0430 now
and the time matters
I'm dreaming work again
hoping that tomorrow
no one will need to do this

but for now
the bees are bees
listening for alarm calls
doing with no significance
though the seams
w o r k e d o u t
while
DREAM WORN
THE LION LISTENS
for alarm calls
ENJUNGLED IN THE NIGHT
AWAKENS
in time
ABOVE
the under

yet the Earth has turned
in the night
and the up may be down
in the morning light

as the

dreamer
stirs
the cauldron of dreams
awaking
to
freedom
and
foolishness

0430 now

and the time matters
I'm dreaming word spam
hoping that tomorrow
no one will need to do this

but for now
the bees are here
looking for dawn calls
doing without significance
that guide names
words glisten
with
THE LN WORD
THE LEON INDEXX
the closer calls
EDUCATORS OF THE NIGHT
MAKERS
of what
LOOT=
for some

yet me I am astounded
in the skies
and the ocean, its doors
to the runaway hulls

as I'm

distant
over
the cauldron of brains
awaking
too
forlorn
out
godliness